BOOK 4

HOME TO THE PRAIRIE

T. L. TEDROW

THOMAS NELSON PUBLISHERS
Nashville

Published in Nashville, Tennessee, by Thomas Nelson, Inc., and distributed in Canada by Lawson Falle, Ltd., Cambridge, Ontario.

While this book is a fictional account of Laura Ingalls Wilder's exploits, it retains the historical integrity of her columns, diary, family background, personal beliefs, and the general history of the times in which she lived. However, any references to specific events, real people, or real places are intended only to give the fiction a setting in historical reality. Names, characters, and incidents are either the product of the author's imagination or are used fictitiously, and their resemblance, if any, to real persons, living or dead, is purely coincidental.

Library of Congress information

Tedrow, Thomas L.
    Home to the prairie / T.L. Tedrow.
       p.   cm. — (The Days of Laura Ingalls Wilder ; bk. 4)
       Summary: While life goes on in Mansfield, Missouri, Laura agrees to help her elderly father fulfill his dream of returning to their former home on the Kansas prairie.
       ISBN 0-8407-3401-8 (pbk.)
       1. Wilder, Laura Ingalls, 1867–1957—Juvenile fiction. [1. Wilder, Laura Ingalls, 1867–1957—Fiction. 2. Frontier and pioneer life—Missouri—Fiction. 3. Fathers and daughters—Fiction.] I. Title. II. Series: Tedrow, Thomas L. Days of Laura Ingalls Wilder ; bk. 4.
PZ7.T227Ho   1992
[Fic]—dc20   92-12763
                                                       CIP
                                                       AC

Printed in the United States of America

2   3   4   5   6   7 - 96   95   94   93   92

Dedicated To

*Sam Moore, who has shown that faith and
determination can move mountains.*

Special Thanks To

*Carla; my wife, best friend, and coauthor.
When the chips were down, she picked them up and
we started again.*

*My four children, C. T., Tyler, Tara, and Travis,
who inspire and help with what I write.*

*My mother, Gertrude Tedrow, who
taught me faith, courage, kindness, love, and understanding.*

*My late father, Richard Tedrow, who told me I could be
anything I wanted. I miss him every day.*

*My sister, Carol Newman, and brother, Richard Tedrow,
who helped me through the hard times.*

CONTENTS

FOREWORD

Laura Ingalls Wilder is known and loved for her pioneer books and the heartwarming television series based on them. Though much has been written about the old West, it was Laura Ingalls Wilder who brought the frontier to life for millions of young readers.

The American West offered a fresh start to anyone brave enough to face the challenges. These people tamed the frontier, crossing the prairie in wagons carrying furniture, seeds, and children, looking for a place to build a new life. They went west to raise families, build farms and towns, churches and businesses. They went knowing they would face hardship and danger, but that those who survived could build a future for their children.

Laura Ingalls's adventures did not stop after she married Almanzo Wilder. She went on to become a pioneer journalist in Mansfield, Missouri, where for sixteen years she was a columnist for the weekly paper, *Missouri Ruralist*.

Laura Ingalls Wilder, a self-taught journalist, always spoke her mind. She worked for women's rights, lamented the consequences of war, and observed the march of progress as cars, planes, radios, and new inventions changed America forever.

While this book is a fictional account of Laura's exploits, it retains the historical integrity of her columns, diary, family background, personal beliefs, and the general history of the times in which she lived. However, any references to specific events, real people, or real places are intended only to give the fiction a setting in historical reality. Names, characters, and incidents are either the product of my imagination or are used fictitiously, and their resemblance, if any, to real-life counterparts is purely coincidental.

T. L. TEDROW

CHAPTER 1

PRAIRIE FIRE

The prairie was alive. Every inch of it seemed to be moving. Thousands of rabbits were hopping madly, tumbling over one another. Prairie hens ran by with their necks outstretched, wings spread, wishing for the gift of flight that would save them.

Laura looked down at the snake wrapped around her leg and kicked madly. It wouldn't let go. Then another snake slithered around her other leg, its tongue going in and out in defiance.

Laura ran screaming through the yard, calling for Pa. "Help, Pa! Help! Get the snakes off me!"

Pa turned for a moment and waved an arm through the thick smoke. He was calling Laura to come—to come help stop the prairie fire that was burning out of control. Everything in its path was being consumed by flames.

Laura looked at the wall of flames encircling her prairie home, and held up her hands to stop it. The fire mocked her futile efforts, showering her with a torrent of cinders.

The air was blackened by thousands of birds flying loops and circles to dodge the burning debris, each one trying to out-scream the deafening wind.

A wet, slithering tongue licked her ankles, and Laura screamed again, trying to pull the snakes off. But they just wrapped themselves more tightly around her legs, their tongues going in and out.

In panic, Laura screamed and tried to pull them off. The snakes just clung tighter, hissing up at her. Laura took an axe handle to beat them from her legs. She didn't care that her ankles were taking most of the hits. The snakes had to come off! They had to come off! After dozens of the most crushing blows that a little girl could manage, the snakes dropped from Laura's legs. She watched them slither away into the smoke.

Her sister Mary ran around the side of the house, screaming, "Indians! Indians are coming!"

From behind the barn, a half-dozen soot-covered braves rode up and halted their nervous ponies. Speaking in their own tongue, they pointed to the black horizon, motioning the Ingalls to come with them.

Not seeing the Indians, Pa shouted from the field, "Laura, Mary, wet down some more sacks! Quick, do it!"

An Indian chief in a singed headdress came galloping to the house and stopped. Laura looked down and screamed. Another snake was crawling up her leg! She screamed again, smacking the axe handle against her ankles.

The Indian chief jumped from his horse and pulled the snake off by the tail. Before the snake could bite, he smashed it against the log wall of the house.

Laura said, "Thank you," but the Indian only nodded a reply. Mounting his horse, he signaled with his hand, and the Indians rode away as fast as they'd come.

"Bring the wet sacks—hurry, girls!" Pa shouted.

Laura and Mary ran to the pile of sacks that Pa and Ma had

laid out next to the well. They each wet down four and dragged them out to where their parents were beating at the flames that were trying to cross the furrow they'd hurriedly dug.

The prairie fire was all around them now, trying to jump over the dirt circle and burn their prairie house down. Suddenly, a flame leaped over, igniting a patch of dry grass. Pa thrashed it out with his sack. "Laura, wet some more sacks! Hurry, girl! Hurry!"

Laura ran as fast as she could. The soot was thick in the air, making her cough and gag. She ripped apart her store-bought slip to cover her face, and she thought her heart would burst.

The prairie fire was screaming louder and louder. It seemed to be shouting, *"I'm gonna burn your house down. I'm gonna burn your house down."*

Laura spun around helplessly. Flames twisted and turned in the air. They danced like whirling devils, flying here and there in the wind. The tips of the flames reached so high that Laura thought they might burn the clouds above.

Laura dragged four more, then six more, then two more sacks over to Pa and Ma. Mary was crying, wanting to hide. "Keep working!" shouted Laura. "Don't be a quitter!"

Baby Carrie was wailing from the doorstep of the cabin, eyes red from the smoke and nostrils filled with soot. Laura took Mary by the shoulders and shook her hard. "Go help Carrie!"

Laura turned in circles. There was no escape. Fire was everywhere. Her parents struggled valiantly to stamp out the flames breaking out all around, but Laura felt helpless. Flames of all colors seemed to reach and grab for her from every direction.

The wind roared louder, and suddenly, a blackened, blinded horse came racing through the flames. He came charging toward Laura, but she couldn't move. Her feet seemed rooted to the ground. As the horse pounded closer, the wind screamed louder. Laura closed her eyes, knowing she was going to die, listening to the hoofbeats pound over the beating of her own heart.

Pa looked over and screamed out, "Jump, Laurie! Jump away!"

Laura opened her eyes at the last moment and fell to the ground as the blinded horse jumped overhead, racing back into the fire from which he'd come.

"More sacks, Laurie—we've got to stop the fire," Pa shouted.

"I'm coming, Pa. I'm coming!" Laura shouted, racing to wet the last three sacks.

"Be quick, Laurie. The fire's gainin' on us," he shouted into the burning wind.

Laura was running her heart out, carrying the sacks, screaming out, "Here I come, Pa. . . . I'm coming, Pa!"

Suddenly Laura was sitting up in her bed, drenched in sweat, still calling out to her father. Her husband, Manly, was holding her in his arms, trying to ease her out of the prairie fire nightmare. "Laura . . . Laura . . . it was just a bad dream . . . just a bad dream," he soothed.

"Oh, Manly, I was just a little girl, and the prairie fire was coming and. . . ."

"You'll be all right," Manly said, patting her like a child. "That was long ago. You're safe now."

Memories of life in the prairie home had been coming back to Laura as thoughts, dreams, and nightmares. Events long forgotten had been pouring from the pockets of her mind since Pa had written that he was coming to visit Apple Hill Farm.

For the first time, he was going to leave his home in De Smet, North Dakota, and come to Mansfield, Missouri, to see what kind of life his pioneer daughter was living. He was going on seventy years old and wanted to see her one last time.

"Oh, Manly, it was so real. The dream was so real," Laura said, sinking against his shoulder.

Manly rested her head back against the pillow, "The mind likes to play with fear. Sometimes it does that when it's bored."

Laura drifted back off to sleep. "It's been so long since I've seen him, Manly . . . so long . . . so many memories."

Manly was saying something, but Laura couldn't hear it. She was back at the prairie house. The blue tobacco of Pa's pipe was tingling her nose.

"Where's my little half-pint of sweet cider half drunk up?" Pa called out from the front stoop, puffing on his pipe.

"Here I am, Pa. Here I am," little Laura shouted out, running to the door. With a single tap on the bottom of his boot, Pa emptied his pipe, then lifted his fiddle from the case. "Play for me, Pa. Please!" Laura begged.

With a smile, Pa said, "Some people play for sad times and some people play for money. Me, why I like to send my fiddle notes to faraway places."

He winked and pointed west. "Laurie, the direction of the setting sun is where the pot of gold is. It's not at the end of no rainbow, it's west . . . in Oregon, where a man can be free."

With bent bow, Pa began the chorus from "Amazing Grace," then stopped, wiping soot from his nose. His face was still streaked with the black cinders of the prairie fire.

"The fire didn't miss us by far, Laurie, but a miss is as good as a mile!"

"It sure is, Pa," Laura said, snuggling against his leg.

"Lookie there, girl," Pa said, pointing to the new moon rising in the sky. "Ol' Mr. Moon beat us this time. There's his campfire."

Laura looked at the shimmering moon and wondered for a moment if it was made of cheese. "Can you eat the moon, Pa?"

He chuckled. "Only if you got a ladder big enough." Digging another deep note out with the bow, Pa smiled. "I'm gonna play one for you, girl."

He looked at Laura and smiled. "Remember, girl, all's well that ends well. That's what a good life's about."

Without an explanation, Pa put his fiddle down.

"Play, Pa, please!" Laura begged.

Pa pulled out his lucky fifty-dollar gold coin and rolled it across his fingers, like a faro dealer in a prairie saloon.

"Charles!" Ma said, shaking her head. "Rolling that coin makes you look like a gambler."

Pa laughed. "Just came honestly to me." He rolled the coin back and forth, moving his hand up and down in front of Laura.

"Let me hold it. Can I, Pa?" Laura squealed with delight.

Pa shook his head. "When I got this in trade for two horses, I thought I'd been took. But this coin taught me that we control our own luck." He flipped it up in the air and winked at Laura. "Lady luck came through for us again," he said. "My lucky gold piece can still work its magic."

He caught the coin with a clap. "Let's see if we'll have luck tomorrow, girl," he said, positioning the gold coin flat on his thumbnail. "Heads or tails? I'll call heads."

"That's what you always call, Pa."

"This coin taught me that you got a choice in life. You either play heads up or land on your tail. I believe in knowin' where I'm goin', so I always call heads."

With a snap of his thumb he sent the coin flipping up toward the star-filled heavens. It seemed to catch the twinkle of the moon.

Pa caught it with a slapping clap and opened his hand. "Aha! Heads it is! We'll have a lucky day tomorrow, Laurie. We're just goin' to have to make it another lucky day."

"But the crops, Pa," Laura whispered, thinking about all that they'd worked so hard for being taken by the fire.

"The luck is that we're alive, girl! There's no great loss without some small gain," he said. "Tomorrow's another day for better plantin'." He leaned over and kissed her cheek. "Just remember that where there's a will, there's a way. Nothin' can stop you if you believe. You got to believe, Laurie . . . will you remember that for me?"

The sweet fiddle notes seemed to bounce off the stars and moon overhead, each low note pushing back the memory of the terrible prairie fire, and each high note bringing hope for a better tomorrow.

Pa moved his head as he played, his tongue licking out some of the hard notes. He looked down and smiled at Laura, a smile that seemed to wrap her in a quilt of love so thick she thought she'd suffocate in wonder.

"I love you, Laurie. I love you," he said, smiling as he moved the bow to the notes. "Sing, girl. Sing it for your pa."

Laura began to sing, moving her head to match the fluid motions of Pa's bow on the fiddle. She drifted away into the past, magnifying the good times, never wanting them to end. *You can go home again,* Laura thought, knowing she was dreaming. *You can go home again—if you believe.*

"I believe," she whispered in her sleep. "I believe."

Manly leaned over and kissed her forehead, wondering why her best dreams and worst nightmares were always about that prairie house.

CHAPTER 2

CHOOSING A MATE

Laura woke up in a wonderful mood. Manly was taking the cows to the far pasture, and Laura just stretched, enjoying the unusually warm February weather.

After the blizzards of December, everyone took the *Farmer's Almanac* seriously when it said it would be cold through May. But by late January of 1906, the ice and snow had melted away, and most of the farmers in Wright County shook their heads and hung the almanac back on the barn nail or outhouse reading post. Even the almanac wasn't perfect.

Laura sat up and reread the letter from her pa. He was coming to visit—his first visit to Apple Hill Farm. Laura couldn't stop thinking about it.

Dear Laurie:

  My feet feel like travelin again. Sellin insurance makes goode money, but it's hard for n old pioneer to talk to folks bout putt in their af-fairs in order. All Ive ever seemed to want to do is put my af-fairs behind me and hit the trail one last time.

  Man weren't ment to live couped up! Livin in one place

*too long is what makes people meen or crazy. That's why
I moved us around so much.*

*So I'm goin to take you up on your offer and come visit
this Apple Hill Farm of yours. I loved the Missoura Ozarks
and from the way you des-cribe what you and Manly have
built, I can already tell you I'm jeallous.*

*Sounds like you've got more than Ma and me and it
took you only a half a lifetime to get it!*

*I hope what I tried to teach you in our wagon jour-neys
helped you some small bit. I know it made you strong,
and I hope your Manly ain't mad at me for makin you
headstrong also!*

*Ma can't be comin cause she's been feelin poorly so I'll
bee catchin the Dakota–Kansas line and arrivin on the
mornin train comin through Springfield on February 7.
I'd walk to you house but my legs aint as good as they
used to be, so I'd preciate you pickin me up.*

*Just want to see my little half-pint of sweet cider half
drunk up, just one last time and talk bout the old days
when life wasnt so dang complicated. Turnin seventy ain't
so much of an accomplisment as it be a durned miracle!*

Love
Pa

Laura smiled at the letter. Pa was a lovable rascal, filled with
the spirit of life. She had never realized how much she missed
him until the letter came. Now he was coming to Apple Hill
Farm on February 7—tomorrow—on her birthday.

She picked up a thirty-five-year-old framed photo of herself
and Pa from the dresser. She had been a little girl with her
strong hero, the man she loved and clung to. The caption in

white on the old photo made her smile. *"Pioneer Pa and His Pioneer Girl,"* she read to herself. *That I was. That I was.*

She could remember that day as if it were yesterday. She was sitting between Pa and Ma on the wagon seat, snug between them—going to town! What a wonderful experience that was.

She was wrapped in Ma's shawl with a blanket tight around her feet, the horses trotting gaily, Pa singing out into the wind, his voice as clear as a summer church bell.

> And we'll rally round the flag, boys,
> We'll rally once again,
> Shouting the battle-cry of Freedom!

"Laurie, we're gonna have two photo-graphs taken—one of the family and one of just you and me. We'll have 'em write on it, 'Pioneer Pa and His Pioneer Girl.'"

"I'm your pioneer girl. I am, Pa," Laura smiled, hugging him.

"I hope you always will be," he smiled, moving the wagon forward.

The memory put a warm glow on the cool February day. Laura dressed and took a cup of coffee with her to the front porch. Manly was walking back through the clearing. The mooing of the cows echoed across the farm.

"Laura, you've got to come see this."

Laura smiled. Every day was special to her husband. No matter how hard times were, he could find a way to push forward. He was just like her father, which may be why she had fallen so deeply in love with him. "What is it, Manly?"

He took the porch steps two at a time and grabbed her hand. "Put that cup of coffee down and come on down to the creek."

The coffee spilled over the rim. "Hold on, hold on. I'm coming," she said, setting the cup on the porch rail.

Manly pulled her along and, even with his limp from the stroke back in the Dakotas, he kept a firm, brisk pace.

"What's got into you?" Laura asked. "You look like you've seen a miracle."

Manly laughed. "Listen," he said, cocking his ear.

Ducks and geese. It sounded like a flock was coming right over the hill toward them. As they topped the hill, he pointed down, whispering, "They've come back early. Means winter's over. No more blizzards or snow."

Below them, the creek and pond were filled with wild ducks and geese, flapping and splashing everywhere. There wasn't a bit of surface that wasn't covered with them.

"What are they doing?" she asked. Manly squeezed her hand and hugged her tight. "Stop that, Manly! I asked, what are they doing?"

"They're courtin'," he laughed.

"Why are they choosing mates now? what's their rush? Spring's not even here yet," Laura said.

"They're choosin' mates for Valentine's Day. Birds choose their mates that day, so they've only got 'bout a week to find one."

Manly scratched his chin and looked back at the pond. "I wonder who's gonna be my Valentine this year?"

"Might not be me if you don't do something special this year," Laura said playfully.

"'Course, if you don't want to be my Valentine, guess I could always ask Mr. Cupid to shoot me a love arrow into someone else."

"And of course, if you did that, I could always take a shotgun and shoot you."

Manly laughed. "Girl, I think you're jealous."

"Just guarding my nest, Manly. Just guarding my nest. Look, Manly, aren't they beautiful?"

Manly turned to see two white swans descending onto the pond. With a flap of their majestic wings, they cleared the ducks and geese away below them and settled down into the center, as if they owned the water. They nuzzled, wrapping their long necks together, kissing with their beaks. It was such a beautiful sight that it took a moment for Laura to speak.

She rubbed her face against Manly's cheek, and they walked arm and arm together back to their nest, back to the house they'd built by hand—a house built with love, devotion, and sincerity.

Apple Hill Farm.

CHAPTER 3

PA INGALLS

He had been on the train for three days, and Pa Ingalls was stiff and sore, feeling his seventy years with every ache and pain. A ten-inch-long square beard hung straight down from his chin, and his wire glasses were bent.

His pipe had gone out fifty miles back, so he packed and re-lit it, drawing deeply. As the blue tobacco smoke curled around his head, Pa fell into the rhythm of the train, watching the Missouri countryside pass by.

Pa knew that life was changing, changing too rapidly for him. It seemed that in the wink of an eye, there were cars, phones, electric lights, and movie houses. *Progress ain't nothin' but a pothole-filled road,* he thought.

He watched the people on the train looking at their pocket watches, preparing for something coming up. None of them even bothered to look at the beautiful countryside. He smiled in irony and wondered, *Why is it that old people seem to enjoy each moment more? Is it because life's clock seems to be ticking faster, telling us to look around, see what we once took for granted?*

Pa had never thought much about his own death, just that it

would come when it would come. But lately, he'd found himself adding up life's events.

He'd done a lot in his life: pioneer, farmer, constable, church elder, carpenter, butcher, justice of the peace, cowboy, deputy sheriff, town clerk, member of the school board, insurance salesman, and even a part-time Republican.

He'd come a long way since being born Charles Phillip Ingalls on January 11, 1836, in Cuba, New York. The third of ten children, Charles first tasted the pioneer life when he was twelve years old and the family moved by wagon to Illinois and then into Wisconsin. At this turning point in his life he fell in love with the freedom of moving on down the road.

Caroline Lake Quiner's father had been lost in a shipwreck, and her mother had remarried a farmer from Connecticut, then moved to Wisconsin with him. Charles and Caroline grew up as neighbors and married in 1860.

Pa shook his head, thinking back to when he and Caroline had lived with his parents for the first years of their marriage. When the families moved by wagon to Pepin, Wisconsin, Charles helped his parents build their big log home and played the fiddle to Caroline in their blanket-walled bedroom.

He told her that they'd have a home of their own soon. "You just got to believe, Caroline—you just got to believe," he told her, digging the bow into his fiddle.

In September of 1863, Charles bought a farm seven miles outside of town and built their first home. When they were finally by themselves, they began a family. Mary was born in 1865 and Laura in 1867. Charles was now Pa—Pa Ingalls.

He laughed to himself, thinking how Laura didn't even know what neighbors were because they were so isolated. She never saw a town until she was four.

Pa watched another tiny town whistle by. The houses seemed unnaturally close together. He had never wanted to live that way and wondered how he'd ended up in a town himself.

"Selling insurance," he mumbled to himself. "Selling durn insurance."

It wasn't like that in the old days. He could remember getting restless in the woods near Pepin, feeling that the neighbors were getting too close when one moved within a mile of their house!

He had gotten antsy, feeling so closed in that he began dreaming of heading west, of going to where a man could stake a claim without sodbusters hemming him in.

Indian country was the best place to go. *Everyone* was talking about it. The white men had broken every treaty they'd written with the Indians, so it was only a matter of time until the Indians would be forced to pack their teepees and move again. Everyone said so.

The small piece of Indian Territory in Kansas had been all but gobbled up by the whites, so Pa wanted to get there before everyone else had claimed all the free land.

His cousin in Washington, D. C., United States Senator John J. Ingalls, encouraged the move, writing him that Indian Territory was open to settlers.

So in the spring of 1870, Pa sold the homestead, loaded his family in a covered wagon he'd gotten in trade, and began the long journey west. Destination: somewhere in the Kansas Indian Territory where the neighbors were far away and a man would not feel so roped in.

They'd spent months crossing the roadless prairies, navigating through the high grass, looking for the perfect place to build a home. Pa had found it in what is now Montgomery County, Kansas. He could remember standing on the bench of their wagon, surveying the land around them. The nearest neighbor was miles away.

He'd taken off his hat and slapped his leg. "Caroline, Mary, Laura—this is where we're goin' to live. This is where we're goin' to build our house."

"Where are we, Pa?" little three-and-a-half-year-old Laura asked.

"On the prairie, girl. We're west of Missouri, north of Texas, and south of the Dakotas."

Pa looked around. There was nothing as far as the eye could see, except tall prairie grass and big sky.

"You gonna build a big house, Pa?" Mary wondered.

Pa shook his head. "We'll start with a small house and see how things progress."

Laura stood up, holding onto his knee, "Will we have real windows and real rooms, Pa?"

Pa dropped his head back, laughing loudly. He picked little Laura up and swung her around. "That's right, Laurie. This is going to be a real prairie home!" Laura squealed with delight and hugged his leg.

Pa closed his eyes on the train, savoring the moment in his mind. He stroked his long, full beard, as if trying to keep the memory going. He saw Laura again, clinging to his knee, asking him to play another fiddle song.

Those were the happy times, before life changed for the worse. He fought back tears, removing his glasses and rubbing his eyes. *Life was simpler then,* he thought. *The best years of my life were those in that tiny prairie house. I wish I could see it just one more time.*

The conductor came barreling through the coach door with

his watch in his hand. "Next stop, Mansfield! Next stop, Mansfield, Missouri!"

Pa adjusted his glasses and picked up his cloth carry bag. A sharp pain shot through his chest and he sat back in the seat, flushed. A thin film of sweat broke out above his lip. With shaking hands, he took out his pillbox and popped it open. Though the doctor had said the pills would help the pain, Pa wanted something to stop the pain. Each one was worse than the last.

This might be the last time I'll ever see my little half-pint of sweet cider half drunk up.

CHAPTER 4

WELCOME TO MANSFIELD

Pa pulled out his lucky gold piece and began rolling it across his fingers. The jolt of the train dislodged his glasses, so he put the gold coin on the seat and pushed his glasses back up his nose, not noticing the coin slide onto the floor.

"Hey, you. Hey, mister," came a young man's voice from across the aisle.

Pa blinked his eyes. "Wha . . . what?" He felt his burning pipe and switched hands, rubbing his slightly burned fingers together.

A young man in his twenties was smiling at him, holding his lucky fifty-dollar gold piece. "You dropped this," the stranger said, handing it to him. Pa took it in his hand while the stranger admonished, "You be careful, old-timer. Most folks would put their shoe on it and keep that piece of gold."

"Thanks," Pa said, rolling the coin on his fingers. The reflection of the morning sun off the gold made him blink, so he rubbed his eyes before looking around to see if he'd dropped anything else.

Laura and Manly were waiting at the station. They turned to listen to the whistle coming from the west, blasting out the train's arrival. The trainmaster walked across the platform ringing his bell. "Springfield to St. Louis, five-minute stop."

"He's coming, Manly. Pa's coming," Laura said, gripping Manly's arm.

Manly looked down the tracks but didn't see anything. "He may have changed a bit now, so be prepared."

Her eyes were glued down the tracks. "Changed? He'll always be Pa," she said. Laura pulled out her pocket watch and checked the time.

"Everyone gets old. Even you will, one day," Manly said, looking at his own pocket watch.

"Pa is Pa," she said bluntly. "Pa's the most gentle, reasonable man I've ever met. That part of him will never change."

As the train drew in, Manly tried to count the cars, but stopped after twenty. People were bustling about in anticipation of the train's arrival.

Baggage and boxes that were being shipped to distant places lined the far end of the platform. An old porter with a handcart moved the bags of the well-dressed Sarah and William Bentley, who controlled the region's timber industry.

"Wonder where they're goin'?" Manly whispered, nudging Laura and pointing to the town's wealthiest residents.

Laura whispered back, "Probably to St. Louis to shop for more clothes."

A group of boys wearing stocking caps pulled way down over their ears ran past, laughing. Manly gave her a questioning look. "Why are those boys all wearin' stockin' caps? Ain't cold enough for that."

Laura shuddered. "Head lice have come round again."

Manly squirmed at the thought of the pesky creatures crawling around on his scalp, and without thinking, he began scratching. "Hate those things."

Laura began nit picking through his scalp. "Got any? Ah, here's one!" she exclaimed, pretending to pull one out.

"Let's see it!" he said in a panic, then saw she was kidding. "Don't kid like that!"

The train brakes were squeaking as the engine chugged to a stop past the platform. Smoke and cinder bits momentarily enveloped the station. Laura coughed, covering her eyes.

A woman with child in hand stepped down carefully from the train, onto the box the trainmaster had set for the passengers. Her child jumped off into the trainmaster's arms.

Pa rubbed his eyes under his glasses trying to focus on the faces in front of him. Everything was unfamiliar. He shook his head, frowning, then held onto the edge of the train car and carefully stepped down, accepting the hand of the trainmaster.

"Pa. Pa!" Laura shouted.

Pa's face brightened. "Where are you, Laurie?" he asked loudly, straightening up and regaining some of his height. He looked around, not seeing her standing there in front of him.

"I'm right here, Pa," she said softly.

Pa dropped his bag and stepped forward at the exact moment that Laura stepped toward him. They caught each other and hugged, losing all time, all age, in that timeless moment.

Laura dug her face into his shoulder and neck, a little girl again, forgetting that she was a mother and almost forty years old. For a moment that passed before she could savor it, Laura was back on the prairie, sitting on Pa's lap. The tower of strength was restored to her life.

Pa's eyes were closed. He hugged her tightly. "My little half-pint of sweet cider half drunk up. I've missed you, Laurie—I've missed you." He pushed her back. "Let me see how you look," he said, smiling at what he saw. "You're still as pretty as a prairie plum."

"Pa, you look great."

He shook his head. "Remember what I taught you 'bout fibbin'?" he said with mock reproach.

Laura smiled. "Yes, Pa, but you do look good."

He smiled. "Can't live forever, but I guess I do look good for seventy." He reached into his bag and pulled out a wrapped gift, creased from travel. He presented it as if it were fresh store-bought.

"What is it, Pa?" Laura asked, feeling like his little girl again.

Pa grinned. "Something for your birthday. It's today, isn't it?"

Manly slapped his palm against his head. "I knew there was somethin' I forgot! Laura, honey, I'm sorry."

"No need to change your ways, Manly. You forgot it last year." Laura smiled sarcastically.

Pa reached out his hand. "Manly. It's good to see you, son."

Laura looked at the package. "You got my card on your birthday, didn't you Pa?" she said.

Pa nodded. "Got it on the eleventh, right on my birthday. But there ain't no sense in celebratin' birthdays when you're old. Just another thing to recall and regret that it passed by so fast."

Laura smiled and grinned at her father. "Pa, your life shouldn't have any regrets."

"Only regret I got now is it's takin' you too long to open this gift!"

Laura felt through the wrapping paper. "Something soft. What it is?"

Pa laughed. "Open it up. It's somethin' I already gave you once."

Carefully taking off the thin red ribbon, tied like a shoelace, she opened the gift. Inside was her first rag doll, aged, but still showing the pencil smile she'd redrawn so many times.

"Oh, Pa!" she said. "Where'd you find it?"

Pa shook his head. "Not me. Your Ma found it. We were goin' through our clothes for the poor box when she found your prairie dolly."

Laura clutched the doll, feeling like a little girl again. "It's wonderful, Pa."

"Brings back good memories, don't it, Laurie?"

"More than you can imagine. More than you can imagine," she said quietly, closing her eyes for a brief moment.

Manly picked up Pa's bag. "Come on, you two. Let's get on back to the farm. I bet you're tired from all that travelin'."

Pa started to grab for the bag, but Manly swung it away.

"Don't be treatin' me like an ol' man."

"Relax," Manly smiled. "You've earned it."

They walked around the small station, to where they'd parked the car. Pa just shook his head at all the hustle and bustle around him. He noticed the boys with their stocking caps and frowned. "You got a cootie outbreak here?"

"Yeah, we do," Manly said. "Those dang lice make me itch, just thinkin' 'bout 'em." Again he scratched his scalp without thinking.

Pa shuddered. "That's all I need. Seventy years old and come home from Mansfield with my head shaved."

They walked a dozen more steps, Pa talking away. "Took me three days to travel what took three months to cover back in the old days." At the edge of the ramp, he stopped and looked around. "You folks sure live in a big city."

Stepping down the exit ramp, Laura laughed. "Mansfield's no big city, Pa. It's big enough to be called a town."

At the street, Pa stopped and caught his breath. A sharp pain had slammed against his chest. He turned away to hide his agony from Laura and slipped one of his heart pills into his mouth without their noticing.

Laura glanced at Manly, then asked, "Pa, are you all right?"

Pa turned back around, took off his glasses, and rubbed his eyes. "Just get short of breath every now and then."

Manly slung the bag into the back seat of Laura's Oldsmobile. She adjusted her skirt and checked her watch.

"Quit lookin' at your watch!" Pa smiled. "You're makin' me feel that I should be boardin' that train, goin' home again!"

Laura grinned. "Sorry, Pa, I was just . . ."

"Just humor your old Pa and quit checkin' the time like it was goin' to stop on you or somethin'."

Manly started the engine. "Next stop, Apple Hill Farm." He pulled back, then started forward with two large backfires.

Pa packed his pipe, struck a match, and pulled deeply. As the blue smoke poured from his mouth in a steady stream, he leaned forward, looking around at the activity on Main Street. "I've seen more automobiles on this one street than we've got in our whole town back home," he said, drawing heavily on the pipe.

"Can't stop progress," Manly shouted over the hello-honk from Dr. George's car.

Laura waved. "The past is past," she said, without turning.

"It's a shame," Pa said, shaking his head.

"What's that?" Laura asked.

Pa took off his glasses and rubbed his eyes. "It's a shame that the future had to come so soon. The past was so good."

CHAPTER 5

LUCKY GOLD PIECE

Pa took out his lucky gold piece and admired the standing Liberty figure on the coin. Without Laura or Manly noticing, he flipped it a few inches in the air.

Heads or tails, he thought, catching it. He decided heads and turned it over. Heads it was.

The reflection of the morning sun off the gold made him blink. He thought back thirty-five years to that day on the prairie when he'd come upon the traveling minister speaking to a few straggly souls at a way station.

Buck Spenser was his name. He was an aging former gunman who'd sent many men to their death but was now preaching salvation, trying to save souls as part of his self-imposed repentance.

Spenser wore a notched, single-action Colt at his side. Solid, sturdy, with a weight of two and a half pounds, Spenser's gun was the same one carried by the other men who'd blazed a path across the West. Men like Billy the Kid, Sheriff Pat Garrett, Bat Masterson, Butch Cassidy, Colonel Bill Cody, and Wyatt Earp.

His Colt six-shooter was known across the West as "The Prairie King"—an equalizer in tough situations, a peacemaker in others and, for thirty men, their last will and testament. Their tombstones were the notches on Spenser's gun handle.

The thirty notches were to remind him of the lives he had taken and the price he would have to pay inside. A debt that had laid heavy on his shoulders since he'd seen the error of his ways.

Charles Ingalls had stopped to listen, just for something to take his mind off his depressing trip to town with twenty-one cents in his pocket. It was just enough money to buy a few chunks of salt pork to keep the family from starving.

The first winter on the prairie hadn't been easy, and the endless sea of prairie grass and harsh times had brought Pa to a crisis of faith. After their house in the Wisconsin woods, living on the open prairie had seemed wonderful. But now just the sight of a tree made him homesick for what he'd left behind.

Pa was looking for a ray of hope for his family. Something to help them make it through. A reason for staying and toughing it out.

Buck Spenser had attracted a small crowd of travelers. Some were just stopping off as part of their endless journey. A few were on their way farther West, and others were hiding from their past.

People on the road were either trying to find something or running away from something. It was a unique part of the American spirit that drove folks to settle the vast open prairie.

Dressed in "preacher black"—from his dusty, peaked cowboy hat to his worn, high leather boots—Buck Spenser looked like a man to be reckoned with. A man to avoid if you could.

Pa could imagine how Spenser faced men down in those Texas towns. Standing in the street, nerves of steel, hand held inches from his holster, giving the other man one chance to draw first.

So Pa stood with the rest of the curious and bored group of tattered stragglers. Men of the cloth came in strange varieties on the prairie and most folks attended the tent and wagon services as much for entertainment as they did for religion.

Buck Spenser looked over the faces and spoke solemnly, "Livin' right is as simple as using a gun. Shoot straight with yourself and you'll never stray. But if you lie to yourself and think you'll just get away with whatever you're doin', then you'll end your days in misery."

An unshaven cowboy guffawed and walked off. Spenser called after him, "You walk off and get yourself another drink . . . you'll need it to stomach what's comin' if you don't change your ways."

A few in the crowd laughed, looked nervously at the dusty cowboy to see if he'd taken insult. But he let it pass, stepped into his saddle, and rode off. Spenser drew his pistol and held it high in the air, scaring the crowd. Then he shoved it back into his holster.

"You don't play with guns—they're dangerous. You load 'em carefully, and shoot 'em only when you need to protect yourself or feed yourself." Buck coughed. "You shoot straight, because you only might get one shot off . . . which is like the chance I'm givin' you to straighten up and live right."

Buck coughed phlegm into a handkerchief, then continued. "My message is as simple as this gun at my side," he said, slapping his holstered Colt for effect. He coughed again, his body racked with agony. "Evil surrounds you every day. It tempts you in saloons and on the streets. So you need to be ready, to be fully armed in your mind to guard yourself from doin' wrong."

He drew his Colt again, brandishing it about. He had such a

fierce look in his red, watery eyes that some in the crowd stepped back.

"This gun spoke but one word . . . death," he said to the hushed, motley group. "Thirty times it spoke and thirty times it delivered someone who'd come after me to where they'd always been goin'."

He lowered his head and spoke in a whisper, "I did what I thought was right . . . like an animal tryin' to protect hisself . . . but I was wrong . . . and I live with it every day . . . but for those thirty men I was dead wrong."

He paused and looked up, gripping the gun. "But at number thirty-one I stopped the killin'. Somethin' came over me to stop my trigger finger from adding number thirty-one to my notches." Spenser raised his hand. "To make up for the bad that I done, somethin' was tellin' me that I had to find thirty people who could make a difference and help change others."

He paused and looked over the small crowd. "Is there one of the thirty here today?" he asked, looking deeply into their eyes. He lowered his head waiting for a feeling, waiting for some message to overtake him. Then he raised his eyes up and focused for a brief moment on . . . Pa.

Pa felt a shiver down his spine and a tingling in his heart, but the feeling passed as quickly as it had come.

"I'm goin' to pass my hat for whatever you can spare. Every penny you give goes to findin' the thirty."

When the hat was passed, Pa gave the twenty-one cents of salt pork money in his pocket. It was all he had, but Buck Spenser had moved him so that he wanted to help this troubled man.

Buck Spenser had seen the prairie man standing on the fringes. By his clothes, he knew that Pa was different from the rest. Not that Pa's clothes were new or fancy, just that they

were clean and patched decently. And he had a look in his eye that said he understood the troubled weight sitting on Buck's shoulders.

"Thank you for the offering," Buck said, shaking Pa's hand and staring into his eyes.

"Wish I could give you more, preacher, but that's all I got to give."

Pa turned to go, but Buck stopped him. "Do you have children?"

"Two beautiful girls and a good woman waiting back at the claim shack for me to return. I'd like to visit a spell, preacher, but I've got to see if I can shoot some dinner on the way home."

Buck Spenser looked into the hat and took out a quarter. "Let me help out . . . it's the least I can do. I'll survive, but it's you who has the mouths to feed."

"No sir, I've learned that faith means doin' what's in your heart. I liked your sermon and gave from my heart."

Buck bowed his head. "You know, it's a rich man who's learned that all the houses, land, or money in the world can't buy a better direction in life than followin' what's in his heart."

"Amen to that," Pa said, turning to leave.

"Wait!" Spenser called out to him, "I've got something for you."

Pa turned. The preacher was fumbling around in his pockets and finally pulled out a shiny gold fifty-dollar piece. "Here, call it and it's yours . . . for your family."

Pa tried to protest, "No . . . I . . . you need it . . ."

Spenser ignored him and flipped it in the air, "Call it. Heads or tails?" Spenser looked into Pa's eyes, "I said call it . . . it may change your life one day."

Pa ignored the irony of the gambling preacher. "Heads," he said as the coin flipped high in the air, turning over and over.

Buck Spenser caught the coin, slapping it onto the top of his left hand. He looked at the coin. "Heads," he said, nodding at Pa and handing him the coin.

A fifty-dollar gold piece was more money than he'd ever held in his life. No matter how badly he wanted it, it didn't seem right.

"I can't take it. It's yours," Pa said, holding out the coin.

Buck refused to take it. "Faith means doin' what's in your heart. I want you to have it."

Pa pushed it on him again. "Use it to find one of those thirty men."

"I'm tryin', but one's not listenin'," Buck said, looking intently into Pa's face.

Pa smiled. "I got to be goin'. Take your gold piece," he said, trying to put it into the preacher's hand.

Buck stopped him with an upright palm. "No, stranger, look at the coin carefully."

Pa turned the coin over and smiled. "Where'd you get this?"

Buck grinned, "A man who lives by the gun walks through the valley of death every day of his life. Got this coin on that road of life I used to lead."

"Then it's special and . . ."

Buck smiled. "I had an innocent man on the street that I'd harrassed for no reason. In my mind, he was ready to be number thirty-one. He challenged me to do what was right and, before I could stop him, he flipped the coin into the air. Said if he called it right, that I should let him go. He called it heads, and I let him go. He gave me the coin to remember him by. I was so shaken by something that came over me that I just uncocked my pistol and put it back in the holster. Never drawed down on a man again."

He patted the pistol on his hip, "Got thirty notches on it. Thirty sins to pay for. Thirty good men to find and touch their lives 'fore I can leave this earth and finally be at peace with myself."

Pa watched as Buck made a cut on one of the notches, turning it into an "x".

"What are you doin'?" Pa asked, fascinated.

"You're number twenty-one. A lucky number from my gambling days. Got only nine more to go," he smiled.

Buck turned and began packing up his sermon papers from the simple, rough-hewn podium he carried with him in his preaching wagon.

"But it's fifty dollars worth of gold!" Pa protested.

"You'll never sell it," Buck chuckled. "Maybe it'll bring you the same luck that it's brought me."

"But, but . . ."

Buck shook his head, "Just keep the secret of the coin to yourself, and one day it will give you a shining moment that will never come again. Then you'll be ready to pass it on."

Pa blinked his eyes at the memory. He was miles from that day on the prairie now, going to his daughter's house.

"We're almost there, Pa," Laura said from the front seat.

"Just take your time. I'm just along for the ride," Pa said, watching the modern world pass him by.

CHAPTER 6

THE YOUNGUNS

"You're pathetic!"

Six-year-old Terry Youngun looked at Uncle Cletus's talking parrot.

"Oh, sure. You're pathetic!"

Terry laughed and mimicked the big green parrot. "Oh, sure. You're pathetic!"

The parrot squawked out, "Taco head!"

Terry shouted back, "Taco head!"

A voice boomed out from the parlor doorway behind him. "Terry Youngun, what did you say?"

Terry turned sheepishly to face his father, Rev. Thomas Youngun, the minister of the Methodist church. "Oh, nothing, Pa. That was just Beezer the parrot talkin'."

"Oh, sure!" Beezer squawked.

"And I suppose that was just Beezer echoing himself?"

"No, Pa."

Beezer interrupted. "You're pathetic!"

They both turned and looked at the bird on the wooden perch. Rev. Youngun shook his head. "Terry, don't go repeatin' what Uncle Cletus's parrot says."

Beezer squawked another interruption. "Say your prayers!"

Uncle Cletus, Rev. Youngun's stuttering seaman brother, who got the parrot in Tijuana on shore leave, came into the room. "Wha . . . wha . . . wha . . ."

Terry moved his head up and down, mouthing the words, trying to help his stuttering uncle out.

"Wha . . . what's goin' on?" Cletus finally blurted out.

Rev. Youngun shook his head. "Cletus, this parrot of yours is a bad influence on my children. Can't you do somethin' to make him not say those things?"

"Oh sure!" the bird squawked.

"Be . . . Beezer! Stop that kind of ta . . ."

Terry blurted out, "Talk!"

"You're pathetic!" Beezer replied, turning a somersault on his perch.

"And you're too much," Rev. Youngun said. He turned to Cletus. "If he's going to stay here while I'm gone, then he can stay in the barn, where his language belongs."

"No, Pa! The cats will eat him!" Terry shouted.

Rev. Youngun stepped from the room. "It's that or get rid of him. I won't stand for that kind of talk."

"Taco head." Before Rev. Youngun could react, Beezer began counting to five in Spanish, *"Uno, dos, tres, cuatro, cinco."*

With his father's footsteps retreating down the hall, Terry shook his head. The thought of being left with Uncle Cletus while his father went across the state to Cape Girardeau on church business gave him a headache.

"You're pathetic!" squawked Beezer, snapping Terry out of his thoughts. "Feed me—feed me—feed me," Beezer screeched.

Behind the barn, nine-year-old Larry and almost-five-year-old Sherry Youngun were sitting on the fence, talking with Maurice Springer, their black friend and neighbor. He was the one they went to for explanations about the mysteries of growing up.

Terry paused at the corner of the barn. Sherry was listening intently, holding onto her Christmas piglet named Little Bessie, who was wrapped in Sherry's blam-blam blankey. Crab Apple the mule was listening over the fence, along with Larry's new horse, Lightning. The barn cat's ears were perked behind Teddy Roosevelt, the turkey they'd named after the president. Dangit the dog had one ear up.

Everybody was listening except Larry, who was preoccupied by the picture he held of Cupid shooting an arrow.

Maurice swatted at Teddy Roosevelt. "Quit gobblin'. You're dinner on two legs." He looked at Larry and Sherry and began laughing. "Church business in Cape Girardeau? That's where that pretty widow named Carla Pobst lives! You sure your daddy's not doin' monkey business?"

"Why?" Larry asked, looking up.

Maurice raised his eyebrows and winked. "Ever since she went back to settle up her affairs, your Pa's been thinkin' 'bout that girl."

"Aren't I his girl" Sherry asked.

Maurice sighed. "It's not quite the same."

"How's it different, Mr. Springer?" Sherry asked, wide-eyed.

Maurice held up his hand. "Girl, you'll understand when you get a valentine comin' after you."

Larry was frowning. Valentine's Day was coming in two weeks, and he was worried. Missouri Poole, the pretty pipe-smoking hill girl in his class, was already making eyes at him. She'd told everyone that Larry was her valentine and they were going to get married. He looked at Cupid and wondered what he'd done to deserve this dilemma. *Heck,* he thought to himself, *I'm only nine years old. Who wants to think 'bout gettin' married?*

But Missouri Poole had told him her mamma got married at twelve and if he wasn't ready to get married yet, he better get ready to kiss her. She had told the entire school that she was going to kiss him on Valentine's Day!

Larry looked at the picture and sighed. "Mr. Springer, why do girls want to kiss boys?"

Maurice chuckled. "Someone been makin' eyes at you, son?"

Larry frowned. "Sort of. I got a girl sayin' I'm her valentine," Larry said.

Maurice smiled. "You gonna give her a valentine?"

Terry stuck his tongue out as if he were gagging. "Why do you gotta give valentines to girls?" sneered Terry. "Why can't you just hit 'em instead?"

Maurice raised his hands. "Boys give valentines to girls and girls give 'em to boys 'cause that's the way it is. One day you'll be old 'nough to understand."

"I don't understand," Terry complained.

Maurice tried to backtrack out of the whole thing. "I was just jokin' 'bout your Pa goin' on monkey business 'stead of church business."

"No you weren't!" Terry said. "Pa hasn't thought straight since he went buggy ridin' with the window . . ."

"Widow," Maurice corrected.

Terry shook his head. ". . . with that widow, and now he's goin' to visit her without takin' us along. Ain't fair!"

Maurice shrugged. "Widow Pobst is a nice woman. She'd make a good momma for you all."

Sherry began crying. "I miss my momma." Maurice picked her up and wiped her tears.

"Is Pa goin' lookin' for a momma for us?" Larry asked.

"Well, no. Maybe." Maurice struggled for words.

"We don't need a new momma!" Terry whined.

"Wish you could be our momma," Sherry sniffled, reaching out and grabbing Maurice's hand.

"Yeah," Larry mumbled. "You're like a momma to us."

"Look kids, a man can't be no momma, so don't be wishin' for what can't be. And I can't be your second daddy. You only got one daddy in this life. I'm just Maurice. I'm your friend."

"But we love you," Sherry said, jumping off the rail into his arms and hugging him.

Maurice smiled at the three of them. "I love you all, too."

Terry hugged Maurice. "You teach us things and talk to us and . . ."

The voice of their father called out from the house, "Larry, Sherry, Terry, time to clean up for supper."

Terry made a face.

"Aren't you hungry?" Maurice laughed.

"Bein' hungry and eatin' Pa's cookin' are two different things."

"And Uncle Cletus's cookin' is worse," Sherry added.

Larry nodded. "He can only cook hard-boiled eggs."

"Hard-boiled eggs? They're good!" Maurice smiled, trying to make the children feel better.

"I'd rather drink the boiled water than eat his eggs," Terry moaned. "You ever eaten yolks so hard you could shoot 'em from a gun?"

Maurice held up his finger. "That's why you need a stepmomma." Rev. Youngun called the children again, and Maurice shrugged. "I think it's time for me to go. You kids best be gettin' on in to supper."

As they ran off he called out to them, "You hear 'bout the city kids from St. Louis comin' here to visit?" Larry stopped, but Maurice waved him on. "Remind me to tell you 'bout it tomorrow. I want you to show 'em 'round my farm."

Rev. Youngun stood on the porch, looking for the first robin of the year. He and his late wife, Norma, had always watched for it together. The noise of the children in the kitchen broke his mood, so he went inside. "Aren't you excited 'bout Uncle Cletus stayin' with you for the next two weeks?" he asked his three children.

"'Bout as excited as we'd be about gettin' the chicken pox," Terry mumbled.

Larry just shook his head, but Sherry said, "Uncle Cletus talks funny. He ta . . . ta . . . ta . . ."

Terry joined in and they both moved their heads up and down, stuttering like Uncle Cletus. "Ta . . . ta . . ."

"Stop it! Yes, he stutters," Rev. Youngun said. "He was born that way and can't help it."

"Why was he born with a shudder?" Sherry asked.

Rev. Youngun sighed. "Stutter, not shudder. It's a speech problem."

"You're sure right he's got a speech problem. Sounds like Crab Apple when he gets a piece of apple stuck in his throat," Terry said.

Rev. Youngun raised his hand. "And that's enough of that. Don't say that around Uncle Cletus. It'd hurt his feelin's."

Uncle Cletus came into the kitchen, rubbing his eyes. "I took a na . . . na . . ."

Terry closed his eyes and said, "Nap!"

"Tha . . . that's right. I fell asleep," Cletus said, smiling.

"Good afternoon, brother," Rev. Youngun said. "You ready for dinner?"

"Wha . . . wha . . . what you makin' to eat, Thomas?" Uncle Cletus asked.

Beezer walked into the kitchen. "You're pathetic!"

Sherry giggled. "Hi, Beezer!"

"Taco head!" Beezer screeched, walking back out of the room.

"Want me to coo . . . coo . . . cook?"

All three Youngun children were standing behind Uncle Cletus, shaking their heads vigorously.

Rev. Youngun ignored them. "Why Cletus, that'd be nice of you. I've got some frog legs soakin' and just need a side dish to go with 'em. What are you goin' to make?"

Cletus smiled. "Har . . . hard . . . hardboi . . ."

Terry and Sherry said simultaneously, "Hardboiled eggs!"

Cletus turned and nodded. "That's right! hardboiled e . . . eg . . . round chicken things."

Rev. Youngun washed his hands and dried them on a towel. "That'd be great. It'll give me time to work on my papers for Cape Girardeau."

Terry shrugged. "Still don't understand why you have to go."

Rev. Youngun shook his head. "Church business. Can't be helped."

"Monkey business, you mean," Terry mumbled softly.

"What, son?" Rev. Youngun asked, checking the kitchen cabinets.

"Nothin', Pa."

"Pa?" Sherry whispered.

"Yes, Sherry?"

"What does monkey business mean?"

Rev. Youngun was caught off guard. "Monkey business? What are you . . . ?" He looked at Terry and Larry, who were edging out of the room. He grabbed them by their collars and lifted them up. "You two boys march to the parlor."

Larry's feet touched the ground, but Terry's legs were too

short and just moved back and forth. Rev. Youngun plunked them down in front of the sofa and sat between them.

"Okay, you two, what's this about monkey business?" Rev. Youngun asked.

"Nothin', Pa," Larry mumbled. "We were just talkin' 'bout things."

"What things?"

Terry moved his feet back and forth, avoiding a direct glance at his father's face. "Just things 'bout the Widow Pobst."

"I see," Rev. Youngun said. "Who's been talkin' to you?"

"Mr. Springer didn't mean no harm, Pa!" Terry said excitedly. "He was just talkin' to us 'bout what you need and—"

"Enough. Enough!" Rev. Youngun said, standing up. "You boys go help your uncle out." He stepped toward the front door.

"Where you goin', Pa?" Larry asked.

"I'm goin' over to the Springers'. Maurice and I got a few things to talk about."

The door slammed loudly. Larry turned and shoved Terry. "Your big mouth got Mr. Springer into trouble."

"We better warn him," Terry said, heading out the back door.

Larry reluctantly followed behind. The two boys took the back trail over the hill, along the creek, and across the ravine, trying to get ahead of their father, who was marching determinedly below them. When their father crossed over the footbridge, they were hopping rocks under it, trying to get ahead and stay out of sight.

At the edge of the Springers' property, the boys cut between the hay bales and sprinted toward the barn they'd seen Maurice entering.

"Mr. Springer! Mr. Springer!" Larry gasped, out of breath. "Terry told Pa 'bout the . . ."

From behind them Rev. Youngun's voice boomed. "About the monkey business I'm goin' to do in Cape Girardeau."

"It wasn't Mr. Springer's fault!" Terry exclaimed, grabbing onto Maurice's leg. "I was just makin' up words and . . ."

Maurice ruffled Terry's hair. "That's okay, son, no need to fib. I said what I said." He looked up into Rev. Youngun's face. "All I can say is sorry. I had no business kiddin' round like that with your kids."

Rev. Youngun frowned. "Just 'cause my church business is takin' me to Cape Girardeau where the Widow Pobst lives doesn't mean that I'm engaging in monkey business." Maurice started to grin, which broke the mood. "You boys go on home," Rev. Youngun said, shaking his head and beginning to smile at Maurice.

At the footbridge, Terry stopped and looked at his brother. "What does Pa need besides us?"

Larry shook his head. "I think it's got somethin' to do with men and women."

"You mean like kissin' stuff?" Terry said, with wide-eyed disgust on his face.

"Think so," answered Larry, remembering Missouri Poole's vow to kiss him.

"Shoot!" Terry exclaimed, kicking at a loose wooden plank.
"What?"

"I hoped it had somethin' to do with cookin'! I'm 'bout starved to death eatin' biscuits so hard you could kill a bear with 'em!" Terry exclaimed.

He stooped down to tie his shoe and found a big green bullfrog that had hopped up from the creek below. Terry put it in his pocket, just doing what came naturally to him.

"Come on," Larry said, "let's go!" The two boys took off, racing back home.

CHAPTER 7

GROWING UP CLETUS

Cletus looked out the kitchen window. It always seemed strange not seeing the horizon move up and down. He'd spent most of the last twenty years at sea, which seemed like home to him.

How did I become a seaman and my brother become a minister? he wondered.

Beezer squawked out, "Say your prayers."

Cletus chuckled and thought, *If my brother had seen the bar in Tijuana where I got that bird, he'd have never let it in the house. That was one knock-down, drag-out fight that night, trying to protect my sailing buddies. But your friends at sea seem like family,* he thought. *They know more about me than my own brother and his family.*

Cletus stopped and sighed. It never failed to amaze him how he could think so clearly in his mind, yet when he tried to talk, the words came out so uncontrollably.

Stuttering is a bad thing to be born with, he thought. *It's a curse that makes people treat you like a fool. They don't know that you're thinkin' straight and the words are there, ready to come out. But the words just don't seem to come out of your mouth like you're thinkin' 'em.*

Cletus walked out onto the porch. It was hard to be around folks, even family, with his stutter. Even his brother, who had protected him from the bullies at school, didn't really know the pain inside.

His parents thought it was something they'd done, then thought that he had suffered some illness. They tried everything, even praying. But the words never rolled off his tongue like the other children's.

Those memories of school were never pleasant for Cletus. Being forced by the teacher to stand and recite simple lines over and over until he wanted to scream.

It wasn't my fault that I couldn't say them! I can't help the way that I speak! he wanted to shout to her.

He could remember shutting his eyes, trying to block out the hurtful stares of the children in the room. They always laughed at him, which was why he never had any friends. His only friend had been his older brother, Thomas.

But even a brother has to go his own way. Though Thomas wanted him to come to divinity school with him, Cletus knew that a stuttering preacher wouldn't be wanted in any church. *Not even a stuttering church,* he smiled to himself. *Even people who stutter don't want to listen to others who do, Because every stutterer is different. There's no rhyme or reason to how things come out.*

So Cletus had gone to sea where he could do his job without having to speak much. Where the other sailors were men like himself, loners trying to escape some hurt from the past.

He loved his brother and his children, and he understood how strange he must seem to them. It was only a few more days until he'd be leaving by train to go back to sea. He could tolerate the embarrassment for that long, then he'd be back in the arms of the ocean where everything was better.

"How's dinner coming?" Rev. Youngun called out from inside the house.

"It's co . . . co . . . coming," Cletus said, struggling over the word.

"Coming right up, you mean," Rev. Youngun laughed, not realizing that behind Cletus' smile was the pain of a lifetime.

CHAPTER 8

APPLE HILL FARM

Manly drove the Oldsmobile across Willow Creek Bridge, listening to Laura and Pa catch up on family gossip. "And what does Mrs. Johnson's twelfth baby look like?" Laura asked.

"As ugly as the other eleven," Pa replied. He shook his head. "You'd think that at least one out of twelve kids would be good-lookin'."

Laura giggled. "Pa, you're exaggerating, aren't you?"

Pa raised his hand in mock indignation. "Laurie, I swear that each of those kids looks like the whole ugly tree landed on his head."

Manly took the turn into the Apple Hill drive. Pa looked around and said, "I hope you're not plannin' to stop and visit some friends. I want to get on and see your home."

Manly stopped at the front steps and turned around. "You're lookin' at it, Pa."

Laura smiled. "Welcome to Apple Hill Farm, Pa."

Pa stared at them both for a moment, then let his eyes roam the house and property. He took off his glasses and rubbed his eyes, then looked around again.

"This ain't no farm," he said slowly. "This is a mansion."

Manly stepped down from the car with that satisfied look a

man gets when his success is acknowledged. "We built it our-selves—from scratch."

Laura accepted Manly's hand and stepped down. "It's taken us over ten years, but . . ."

"But nothin'," Pa exclaimed. "You got more house and spread here than anyone else back home."

Manly reached out his hand to help Pa down, but Pa spurned it. "I can get myself down, Manly Wilder. From the looks of this place, you've done wore yourself out!"

Pa stayed on the porch and looked around while they carried his bags in and put them in the guest room. He was deeply impressed, proud, and somewhat humbled by what lay before him.

He turned as Laura swung the porch door open. "You want some coffee, Pa?" Laura asked, checking her pocket watch.

"That'd be nice. What's Manly doin'?"

"He's just going to feed the livestock," Laura answered, look-ing at her watch again. "I'll go get that coffee now," she said, letting the door close quietly behind her.

Pa stepped carefully down the porch steps and headed toward the path up the ravine. He walked the property until he came to the top of the hill above the house.

From behind, Laura approached with two cups of coffee in her hand. "Penny for your thoughts."

Pa turned. "Oh, I was just thinkin' 'bout the house in Kan-sas."

Laura handed him the coffee and smiled. "I think about it a lot."

Pa put his arm around her shoulders. "Lordy, I'd love to see the old place just one more time. Feel the walls I cut and the furniture I made for your Ma."

"It'd be nice, wouldn't it?" she said, closing her eyes.

"Just one more time," Pa mumbled to himself, "that's all I ask. So I can figure a few things out."

"Like what, Pa?"

Pa sighed. "Like why things seemed to be going so good and went so bad. I'm haunted by the what-ifs. What would our lives have been like if we hadn't been forced to move? Or what if we'd stayed in Wisconsin and never moved to the prairie at all?"

"Can't change the past, so you shouldn't worry yourself over it."

Pa shrugged. "Easy for you to say, 'cause I'm the one who made the mistakes. Our prairie home was my favorite house of all. I'd just like to touch it again, to see if it will settle the haunts in my mind."

Laura looked into her father's eyes. "Can you really go home again, Pa?"

He nodded thoughtfully. "I don't think I've ever really left it, the way my mind's been actin' up about it."

Laura absentmindedly started pulling her pocket watch out, but Pa pushed her hand away. "Laurie, you got to stop countin' the minutes. Sometimes you got to stretch the moment, make it last."

"Yes, Pa," she said in a little-girl tone, nestling into his arms.

"That's better. You listen to your old pa a bit and you'll see that what you gain by rushin' is lost by missin' the beauty of the moment."

He closed his eyes for a moment, then opened them on a breathtaking sight. "Look," he said, pointing to the two swans flying through the air in beautiful, synchronized movements. "What a picture that would make."

"Aren't they beautiful?" Laura whispered, watching the swans turn a figure eight in the air.

"That's what life's all about, Laurie," Pa said quietly, "not sacrificing what you have for what you think you're goin' to have." As the swans flew off, he added, "Took me a long time to learn that, believe me."

After dinner, they all sat on the front porch, drinking coffee and enjoying the end of the day. They talked about how Rose was doing at her New Orleans high school and when she was coming home again.

"Well," Pa began, slipping down in his chair, "I told Laurie that I'd like to go back into Kansas and see our prairie house, the one in Indian Territory that we had to leave."

Laura stopped him. "I know, Pa, but we'd never be able to find where it was."

Pa reached into his pocket and pulled out a crumpled, folded piece of paper. Unfolding it, he spread it out on the railing before them. Laura immediately recognized the aging, faded, hand-drawn map. Pa had carried it across the prairie, charting their course by the stars and this special map. For a moment she could almost feel the Kansas wind blowing through the tall grass that covered the seemingly endless, flat land.

"It's right there," he said, pointing to the map.

"What's right there?" Manly asked, leaning forward.

"Our house," Pa said, looking sharply at Manly.

Laura took Manly's hand. "Pa's talking about the prairie house. Right, Pa?"

"That's right, Laurie! It's right here. Right under my finger."

Manly picked up the map. "You sure?"

"Sure I'm sure," Pa said indignantly. "I picked the spot out in the first place."

Manly put the map down. "Where'd you get this map? It says 'Indian Territory.' Heck, that was changed almost thirty years ago."

Laura took the map from Manly's hands and looked at it. "Pa, this is the trail from Pepin."

Pa smiled. "That's right. Drew this line when we were headin' toward the prairie from Pepin. It's got all my special codes and landmarks I was lookin' for and some I made along the way."

Laura traced her finger along the paper. Somewhere in her mind, she could remember Pa showing the map to her grandmother in Wisconsin. All the uncles were gathered around, helping load the wagon and hitch the horses.

The cousins had kissed one another, and then Pa set her and Mary in the back of the wagon. They were on their way to Indian Territory. Pa was laughing from the front of the wagon. "I'm gonna show you a papoose when we get out West."

"What's a papoose, Pa?" little Laura had asked him.

"A papoose is an Indian baby. The Indians out there are nice. I think we're gonna like meetin' 'em."

Pa tapped Laura on the arm. "Are you daydreamin' or somethin'? Hand me the map, please."

Laura smiled and handed him the map. "Guess I was just thinkin' about our travels back then."

"Why'd you pick now to want to go?" Manly asked.

Pa looked from face to face, then said, "Because I probably won't have another chance to get back there. I'm gettin' old, Manly."

"The whole idea is silly!" Manly laughed. "You'd never be able to find it!"

Pa shook his head. "I found it the first time, and I can find it again," he said.

"All I'm sayin' is times and places change," Manly chuckled. "Heck, there could be a city or two-lane road built right over the place."

Pa held up his hand for silence. "I'd just like to see the place one more time, that's all," he said, looking off.

"So would I," Laura said, trying to placate him.

Pa's eyes brightened. "You would? Then why don't you come with me?"

"What? What are you talking about, Pa?"

"I'm talkin' 'bout goin' home one last time. That's why I only booked a one-way ticket on the train. I'm goin' to get me a wagon and team of horses and go find the old place."

"By wagon?" Manly exclaimed. "You can't do that!"

"You just watch me," Pa said, folding his arms.

"You're gettin' too old for that." Manly looked at Laura. "Tell your pa to give up this idea. It's crazy!"

Pa grabbed Laura's hands and looked into her eyes. "Come with me, Laurie. We could go together by wagon."

"Not on your life," Manly said, putting his foot down. "It's a crazy idea."

Pa set his jaw. "I'm goin'. Alone or with one or the both of you, I'm goin'."

Manly stood up and started inside. He turned at the door. "I think everyone needs a good night's rest to forget this foolish talk. Pa, I'll take you to the train station tomorrow so you can buy the other half of your ticket."

Pa mimicked Manly as the door closed, " '*Pa, I'll take you to the train station tomorrow*'—who does he think he is? My wet nurse?"

Laura giggled. "He means well, Pa. He's just concerned for you."

"Let him be concerned 'bout his own self. I'm goin', and that's all there is to it." He walked over and pulled Laura to her feet. "Little half-pint of sweet cider half drunk up, are you comin' with me?"

She looked into his eyes. "Let me think about it. Okay, Pa?"

He smiled and shook his head as if his whole world had suddenly changed. "You never had to think 'bout it before. You were always the first into the wagon, lovin' life on the prairie."

"Everyone and everything changes, Pa," she said quietly.

"True spirit never changes. Even in these ol' bones, I've still got the spirit of a young pioneer." He started down the stairs, then looked into her eyes. "You had it once, Laura. You *were* my pioneer girl." He stepped off the last stair and walked off alone, leaving the lingering aroma of his pipe to tingle her nose.

"I still am," Laura whispered. "I still *am* your pioneer girl."

CHAPTER 9

EVENING SONGS

As evening descended on Apple Hill Farm, Laura was caught up in a jumble of emotions. Seeing her father and thinking about their lost house had brought back joys and heartaches that had been covered over in her mind.

Laura drifted off in thought, remembering leaving their Kansas home as if it were just yesterday. She hadn't known where they were going, only that Pa had sold the cow and the calf and they had to leave.

She and Mary were holding onto baby Carrie in the back, all of them dressed in fresh-washed clothes. *I don't want to leave. I don't want to leave,* she thought.

Pa tightened the ropes on the back of the wagon, blocking her view. "Let me look back, Pa. *Please let me look back.*"

Pa shook his head. "Lookin' back too much can make you think you're goin' in a wrong direction in life."

"Please, Pa—just one look," she pleaded.

"All right, Laurie. Just one look back."

Pa opened the back of the wagon and Laura kept her chin on the edge as their home faded into the distance. The house seemed to be calling out to her, *Please don't leave. Please come back.*

Then Pa was fiddling to the endless sky, raising his voice, trying to raise their spirits:

> *Row away, row o'er the waters so blue,*
> *Like a feather we sail in our gum-tree canoe.*
> *Row the boat lightly, love, over the sea;*
> *Daily and nightly I'll wander with thee.*

Laura was so deep in thought that for a moment, she swore she could hear again those sweet fiddle sounds that moved her so. Was she dreaming, or was she hearing things? Opening her eyes, she turned her head to the sounds about her.

Birds chirped their good-byes to the day. The first crickets of the evening scratched away. Ducks called from overhead. A cow mooed, and a horse whinnied.

Then she heard it: clear as a prairie evening from long ago, Pa's fiddle notes echoing out through the ravines and ridges, bouncing off the trees and dancing with the wind.

The sound was coming from the top of the orchard hill. "Pa," she whispered. "Pa's playing my song."

Without hesitating a moment, she picked up her skirt and rushed up the slope. With each step, the sound grew louder, and as she stepped behind the large boulder at the highest point, she came upon Pa, sitting on the edge of the outcrop, playing to the beauty before him.

He looked like a man in some fairy-tale time and place, sitting on the edge of the earth, hitting sweet notes of praise for the magnificence about him. His eyes were closed, and his lips silently mouthed the words to the song.

He hadn't noticed Laura. She listened for a moment, then stepped toward him, singing the song. When he heard her voice, he turned without stopping, digging the fiddle bow deeply into each note to accent her high-pitched voice. For a golden moment they were lost in their memories, thinking about a time and place long ago. At the end of the song, she clapped, and he slightly bowed his head.

"Didn't know you were listening," he said, trying to unbend a kink from his bow arm. "Every time I hear the evening animals strikin' up before a beautiful sunset, I just have to play."

Two geese flew honking overhead, and the crickets seemed to call out for another song. Smiling and winking at Laura, Pa played the chorus from "Amazing Grace."

"Oh, Pa, I just love that hymn."

Pa stopped, keeping the bow on the fiddle. "It was your favorite on the prairie."

"Sometimes those days seem so far away, and sometimes they seem to be right at the tip of my fingers."

Pa hugged her tightly. "How 'bout another fiddle song?"

"Just play 'Amazing Grace' as we walk back to the house."

Pa started to play, then felt a sharp pain across his chest. He caught his breath, holding his hand over his heart.

Laura was startled. "Pa, what's wrong? What's wrong, Pa?"

Not wanting Laura to see the medicine, Pa turned from her and slipped a pill into his mouth. Slowing his breathing down, he closed his eyes for a moment until the pain subsided. "It's nothin'. Just get these pains every now and then."

He straightened up and hit a note on his fiddle. With a big smile he said, "Your Pa's just gettin' old. That's why I want to go now to see our house again . . . before my time is up."

Before she could respond, he dug out the first notes of the song and played his heart out as they walked back to the farmhouse.

At that moment, Laura knew she wanted to go with Pa.

When they reached the porch, Pa shook his head. "Go on in. I want to be by myself for a bit."

"You sure?"

"I'm sure. Go on in now and be with Manly."

Three steps from the stairs he disappeared into the descending darkness, pipe in one hand, fiddle in the other. Laura tried to find him in the evening shadows. Then she saw the match strike on his boot as he up his pipe. The faint smell of the burning tobacco drifted around her as it had done so many nights on the prairie.

CHAPTER 10

FROG LEGS

Sherry was in the kitchen, singing off key. Uncle Cletus ignored her while he prepared supper for the Youngun family. A dozen eggs were in a basket, waiting to be hard-boiled. Fresh, just-gigged frog legs were soaking in a bowl, courtesy of a church lady.

Sherry paused for a moment to catch her breath. Uncle Cletus sighed, thinking she had finally stopped, but she began to sing even louder.

Uncle Cletus just clenched his jaw and ignored the grating, off-key high notes. Finally she stopped and tugged at his sleeve.

"Uncle Cletus, do you know the Peter Piper rhyme?"

He started to stutter an answer, then just nodded his head yes. He knew it—had never been able to say it, but he knew it.

Sherry clapped her hands. "Oh, goody! Let's see who can say it the fastest and bestest!"

Before Uncle Cletus could stop her, she stood up on her chair and began. "Peter Piper picked a peak—no, that should .be—Peter Piper pricked a peck of peppers pickled." She frowned. "Two mistakes and I'm out. Your turn, Uncle Cletus."

He closed his eyes and sighed at the dilemma his stuttering always placed him in. Wiggling his jaws around, preparing to sound out each word carefully, he began slowly. "Pe . . . Peter Piper pic . . . pic . . ."

Sherry clapped her hands. "My turn!" Uncle Cletus looked flustered, but she began again. "Peter Piper picked a peck of pickled peppers. A peck of pickled peppers Peter Piper picked."

She stopped and caught her breath, wrapped up in the enthusiasm of the moment. "If Peter Piper picked a peck of pickled peppers, where's the peck of pickled Peters that Peter Pepper picked?" She hit her fist into her hand. "I messed it up. Your turn."

Wiping his hands, he took a deep breath and began very slowly. "Peter Piper picked a . . ." He hesitated at the next word and gulped, "Peck of." He looked very relieved that he'd gotten each word right so far.

"Go on. You're doin' great!" Sherry said.

Uncle Cletus kept going. ". . . pickled pe . . . peppers. A peck of . . . pickled pe . . . pe . . . peppers Peter Pi . . . Piper picked. If Peter Piper picked a pe . . . pe . . . peck of pickled peppers, where's the peck of pi . . . pickled . . ."

He slowed down to a crawl to get each last word right. ". . . peppers . . . Peter . . . Piper . . . pi . . . pi. . . ."

Sherry was nodding her head up and down, mouthing the words along with him. Uncle Cletus caught his breath, ". . . pi . . . pi . . . *picked!*" He mouthed. "I did it. I did it!" Then he screamed out, "I did it!"

Sherry jumped down, clapping her hands, and hugged his legs. "You did it, Uncle Cletus!" Sherry stood back, all aglow with the excitment of the moment. "Now, let's do Peter, Peter, Pumpkin-Eater."

Uncle Cletus shook his head. "N . . . no! I've got to coo . . . coo . . . cook dinner!"

Sherry took a fork and poked at the frog legs in the bowl. "How do the frogs get around without their legs?"

He sighed. "They do . . . don't. They're dead."

"Oh," said Sherry, solemnly. "What does 'got a frog in your throat' mean?"

"I do . . . don . . . don't know," he said, shaking his head.

"Terry says that if you eat frog legs you'll croak. Is that true?"

Cletus chuckled. "No."

She looked at the soaking frog legs. "They almost look alive, don't they?" She didn't like frogs or the thought of eating their legs.

Uncle Cletus sprinkled salt in the bowl, and the legs began to wiggle around. Sherry put her hands over her eyes and ran from the kitchen, screaming.

Uncle Cletus chuckled to himself, "Thought you knew how to make the frog legs ju . . . jum . . . hop!"

At dinnertime, Rev. Youngun looked at his fresh-scrubbed children and smiled. "Who would like to say the blessin'?"

As usual, only Sherry raised her hand. "All right, Sherry, you may say it. Hold hands, everyone."

Sherry took a deep breath. "Thank you for the hard-boiled eggs and . . ."

Terry stuck his tongue out, pretending to gag at the thought of the eggs. He caught the glare from his father and quickly bowed his head.

Sherry continued. "And for the bowl of slimy green frog legs, and for bringing Uncle Cletus to visit with us. Amen."

As the eggs were passed, the kids stared at them sitting starkly on their plates. "Okay," Rev. Youngun said, "let's crack the eggs."

Uncle Cletus picked up his egg and, without any warning,

cracked it on his brother's head. Rev. Youngun looked startled, but then smiled.

"That's what you always did to me as a boy!"

Rev. Youngun took his own egg and cracked it lightly on his brother's head.

"Did it hurt?" asked Larry.

"Not at all," his father answered, smiling at Cletus.

Larry cracked his egg on Terry's head, and Sherry cracked hers on Larry's head. Suddenly, Sherry saw the look on Terry's face as he tossed his egg back and forth in his hands, moving his eyebrows up and down.

"Pa! He's goin' to crack my head!"

Rev. Youngun looked at Terry. "Not too hard, son. You don't want to break the egg in half."

Terry made a wild motion, circling his arm around. Sherry closed her eyes. Terry swung his hand toward her head with brute force, then pulled back at the last moment, just barely tapping the egg on her head.

"See? I wasn't goin' to do it hard," Terry said to her in a soft voice.

Sherry looked relieved. "Thanks, Terry."

The moment she turned to get salt for her egg, Terry's arm went up like a cobra's head and came down with a loud cracking sound on her head. Only this egg wasn't cooked—it was raw.

Everyone sat open-mouthed as the big yellow egg yolk ran between her eyes. Sherry's eyes welled, and her lips began to quiver.

"I . . . I . . . didn't know it was . . ." Terry stammered. Sherry's piercing scream shattered the room. "Sorry, Sherry, sorry," Terry said, trying to stop her crying. "I didn't know it wasn't cooked!"

Uncle Cletus blushed and said sheepishly, "I knew there was one I didn't cook."

Rev. Youngun wiped the yolk off Sherry's face, carried her to the sink, and cleaned her up, then sat back down and tried to resume dinner.

Beezer watched from the sideboard, scratching his underbelly on the edge of the silver tray.

Sherry got up and imitated Beezer. Rev. Youngun was not pleased. "What *are* you doin'?"

"Imitatin' Beezer," she giggled.

"Cletus," Rev. Youngun said, glaring at his brother, "does this parrot have mange or somethin' catchin'?"

Cletus shook his head. Uncle Cletus picked up the serving plate of frog legs and took two for himself. He held the plate out to his brother, who took two fat ones.

"Nothing like really fresh frog legs, eh, Cletus?"

Ribet, ribet.

Everyone looked at each other, wondering whose tummy had made the funny sound. Larry shrugged his shoulders. "It's not me."

Ribet, ribet.

Terry sucked his breath in. He'd forgotten that big green bullfrog he'd picked up at the creek was still in his pocket. With one eye he looked down. The frog was staring back up at him from his pocket.

Ribet, ribet.

"Are you makin' that sound, Terry?" his father asked.

"No, Pa, it's not me," Terry said truthfully.

Larry eyed the fried frog legs. "Church lady said they were fresh, Pa."

Ribet, ribet.

Larry looked at them closely. "Must be *real* fresh, Pa."

Ribet, ribet.

Uncle Cletus looked at the plate of cooked frog legs and shrugged his shoulders. Beezer made a disgusting noise.

Rev. Youngun looked relieved. "It must have been Beezer makin' the noise."

"Oh, sure!" Beezer squawked, making the kids laugh.

Cletus just nodded and passed the plate to Terry. The frog he'd picked up earlier was wiggling around in his pocket, so he took the plate with one hand and pulled the frog out under the table with the other.

Everyone was watching Beezer do his scratch dance, so Terry quickly placed the big, green bullfrog on the serving plate and handed it to his sister. "Here's your fresh legs, Sherry."

Sherry turned and went white as a ghost. *Ribet, ribet,* went the big bullfrog. Sherry fell over backward, screaming, and the platter crashed on the floor.

Rev. Youngun, who had been watching the silly parrot scratch himself, turned around, muttering, "What the—" Sherry took a swipe at the frog, who landed on her father's plate.

Ribet, ribet.

Rev. Youngun knew immediately who the culprit was. "Terry, get your frog out of here!"

"Mine, Pa?" Seeing the look of fury in his father's eyes, Terry knew that getting out of this one was hopeless. "Yes, Pa," he said loudly, grabbing the frog. He ran to the back door and tossed it outside.

Ribet, ribet, ribet, ribet. The sound of the frog slowly faded away as it hopped back to the creek.

Uncle Cletus was giggling, sucking the meat off a fat frog leg. "Got an . . . an . . . anymore legs?" Everyone dumped legs on his plate.

After dinner, Rev. Youngun stood on the front porch, watching the sunset. "I miss you, Norma," he whispered to the sunset. "These kids need a stepmomma. I hope you understand."

A red robin landed on the rail next to him, twisting and turning his head. The bird stopped for a moment, nodded up and down, and flew off.

Rev. Youngun shook his head, a slight grin on his face. "Thank you for understanding, Norma. I'll always love you. No one could ever take your place in my heart."

CHAPTER 11

THE YOUNGUNS' SONG

Rev. Youngun put down his pencil and rubbed his eyes while dimming the light. There was church business in Cape Girardeau, and there was the Widow Pobst. He was troubled by what people would say if Maurice joked about his trip. Should he tell the deacons of the church, he wondered? Should he cancel the trip? He'd worked long and hard to earn the respect of his congregation, and everything he'd done could be dashed away if people started thinking that he was going on "monkey business" instead of church business. It was a church meeting he could miss, but then he'd also miss seeing Carla Pobst, who'd written that she'd like to see him and take a buggy ride when he came to town.

He couldn't think straight. All he could think about were her dark hair and fiery eyes. Feeling like a teenager again, he carried her letter around in his pocket. Everything was so jumbled up that it was hard just to get his socks on right. He found himself thinking about her at the oddest moments and smiling at the wrong times.

Rev. Youngun found Sherry in the upstairs hall and scooped her into his arms. "Let's sing our song," he whispered into her ear.

"Okay, Daddy," she giggled.

They looked into each other's eyes and whispered the words, kissing lightly after every "will ya":

> *Give me a little kiss, will ya? Will ya? Will ya?*
> *Give me a little kiss, will ya?*
> *I . . . love . . . you.*

They hugged, laughing together, and he carried her into the boys' room. "Ready to sleep, boys?"

"Ah, Pa, it's too early!" Larry moaned. "I haven't fed my spiders or snakes yet."

Terry fell backward on the bed. *"Feed 'em Sherry.* That'll give 'em in-die-ges-tion for sure!"

"Pa!" Sherry screamed, "Terry's bein' mean!"

"Children, let's not argue before bed," Rev. Youngun said. "Let's sing the 'Younguns' Song.' Your mother wanted you to sing it every night. Come on, sit up."

Larry sat up straight, but Terry barely raised his head. "Come on, Red, get up," Rev. Youngun said, pulling on him. "Larry, you start it."

Larry cleared his throat and quietly began. They all joined in:

> Brother to brother,
> Father to son,
> Thank God for blessin'
> The Youngun children.

> Now mother to daughter,
> Mother to son,
> Thank God for blessin'
> The Youngun children.

Larry paused for a moment and reached for Terry's and his father's hands. Terry took his hand. When he hesitated at holding Sherry's hand, a stern look from his father ended his rebellion.

> Join hands together,
> The family is one;
> Thank God for blessin'
> The Youngun children.
>
> And now that we lay our . . .
> Selves down to sleep,
> Thank God for blessin'
> The souls that he keeps.

The children dropped hands and snuggled down. Rev. Youngun stood up to take Sherry to her room. "Good night, boys. Good night, Larry. Good night, Terry."

"'Night, Pa. 'Night, Sherry," Larry said.

"'Night, Larry. 'Night . . ." Sherry looked at Terry, who was sticking his tongue out. "'Night, Terry."

Rev. Youngun looked at Terry, "Well?"

With a resigned shrug, Terry said quickly, "NightPaLarrydumbSherry."

From the doorway of Sherry's bedroom, a pink snout peeked out. Sherry slipped from her father's arms and grabbed up her pink piglet, Little Bessie.

"'Night, Pa," she said from the darkness of her room. "'Night, Momma. I miss you."

Rev. Youngun closed his eyes for a moment, feeling he might burst from the emotions that were tearing him apart.

CHAPTER 12

GAMES

That night Laura fell deep into dreams about the house in Indian Territory. The dark, gray prairie sky hung all around her. The world seemed bleak. Rain was falling, and hard bits of snow were in the air.

Inside, the world was glowing. Pa was cleaning rabbits by the warm glow of the fireplace, while Ma pieced a patch quilt.

"Let's play a game," Mary said to Laura.

They played Pat-a-Cake, Hide the Thimble, and Cat's Cradle.

Pa laughed from the corner. "There's a game you can play about Ma's supper."

"What is it?" Laura asked.

"We're havin' bean porridge and salt pork for dinner."

The girls laughed and began playing Bean Porridge Hot, clapping their hands together, trying to keep time while they said the rhyme:

> Bean porridge hot,
> Bean porridge cold,
> Bean porridge in the pot,
> Nine days old.

Some like it hot,
Some like it cold,
Some like it in the pot,
Nine days old.

I like it hot,
I like it cold,
I like it in the pot,
Nine days old.

Pa chuckled. "That's one thing you'll never taste. Your Ma's bean porridge is so good that it's never lasted more than two days!"

The wind screamed outside. Everything good was within the walls, and the big, bad world was beyond them. But Indian drums pounded in the distance, seeming to cry, *Get out. Get out.*

Pa checked his rifle and the bolt on the door, then went back to cleaning the rabbits.

"Are the Indians playing games, too, Pa?" Laura asked.

Pa's expression changed. "No, Laurie, I don't think they're playin' games. I think they're deadly serious."

CHAPTER 13

THE FIRST WINTER

Pa had slept peacefully, rising well before dawn, eager to start the day. He'd dreamed about hitting the road again. Every fiber in his body tingled with excitement.

He might be seventy, but he felt like forty again as he looked in the mirror. His long, rectangular beard made him frown. *An old man's beard,* he thought.

Without a second thought, he searched around the dresser, finding an old straight razor and whetstone. He looked in the mirror at the beard he'd worn off and on for most of his adult life and breathed deeply.

"Ain't seen my face in a long time," he chuckled, dipping his hands into the cold water bowl. He wet his face and did his best to lather up the beard, but it was too long and thick.

Digging around in the dresser some more, he found a pair of scissors. Taking the end of his beard in one hand, he pulled it straight and cut it off around his chin. When he was finished, he held a ten-inch matt of salt-and-pepper beard.

"Looks like a bird's nest," he laughed, opening the window and tossing it out. A small, brown bird landed on the roof and flew off with a strand of it.

Pa laughed and admired his handiwork in the mirror. With

quick strokes, he sharpened the razor on the whetstone. It was soon sharp enough to take off the remaining hair and left only a few cuts and nicks on his face. When he was finished, Pa looked in the mirror again and saw the lower half of his face, which he hadn't seen for more than ten years. With just a drooping mustache left, he looked twenty years younger!

Straightening up, he stretched and began thinking thoughts that hadn't been on his mind in a long time: prairie days and prairie nights, the freedom of the road, hunting dinner, hugging his woman by the campfire.

"If Caroline were here right now, why I'd . . ." he laughed loudly. "I'm actin' like a kid," he chuckled, pulling on his jeans, boots, and wool shirt.

Stepping as quietly as he could, Pa opened the front door and stood on the porch. Dawn was dancing on the horizon. Creatures of the dark were saying their final good nights, and the day players were talking their heads off, looking for breakfast.

Pa's rambling around the kitchen awakened Manly. He looked at the clock. Five-forty-five. Laura was sleeping peacefully, but Manly, irritated, tapped on her shoulder.

"What? What is it, Manly?" she grunted, blinking her eyes.

"He's up."

"Who's up?"

Manly sat up on the edge of the bed. "Your Pa is up, rattlin' around downstairs like a raccoon."

From below them, Pa's voice boomed out, "You lazyheads gettin' up? It's almost six! Time to rise and shine!"

Manly turned to Laura and said, "I wish he was back on the prairie right now."

Laura giggled. "You tell him that and he'll be gone before sundown."

"Don't tempt me. Don't tempt me," Manly said, heading toward the door.

Laura slipped on her robe and wool socks and padded quietly down the stairs. "Morning, Pa," she said to her father's back. Pa was looking in the icebox and didn't respond, so she said it again. "Morning, Pa."

Pa turned. "Oh, morning, Laurie. Didn't hear you. Men lose their hearing 'fore women. Your Ma's always gettin' on me to listen more—" Laura was staring at his clean-shaven, nicked chin. "What's wrong? Cat got your tongue?"

"No, Pa, it's just . . ."

Pa felt his chin and laughed loudly. "I shaved. You ain't seen my face since almost 'fore you got married."

Laura shook her head. "It gave me a startle, all right. What got into you?" she asked, walking up for a closer look.

Pa jutted his chin in and out. "Oh, just got up with the travelin' feelin'. All that talk has got me antsy to hit the road again."

"Oh, Pa," she said, hugging him, "it's fun to dream, isn't it?"

Pa pushed her away, "This ain't a dream. I know you'd like to go cross that prairie again, and you know it, too."

"We'll talk about it later," Laura said, tightening her robe. Pa shook the cereal bag. "What are you doing?"

He looked back into the icebox and shook his head, smiling. "You got enough food in here to feed an army."

Laura nodded. "I just like having food on hand. I don't like feeling hungry or worrying about having enough to eat."

"We had hungry days, didn't we?"

"Some of those hungry times are in my dreams at night, Pa."

"Mine too," he said, sitting down at the table. "Do you remember when the first crop didn't take and the cabin still had an earthen floor?"

Laura had been little then, and she only vaguely remembered it. "Tell me, Pa. Maybe it's what I dream about."

Pa sipped his coffee and began. "Caroline—er, your ma—was worried whether we'd have enough food to last that first winter in the Indian Territory. I tried to calm her fears, but there was little game to be found.

"Ma didn't want you girls to worry and never wanted you to forget your manners, so even with that last loaf of bread and the few scraps of hardtack we had left in my rucksack, we gathered at the table like a family. You were sayin' the blessin', Laurie, when someone knocked on the door.

"Before I could open it or reach for my rifle, an old Indian came in. His hand was outstretched, pointin' to his mouth and stomach, tryin' to make me understand. 'He's hungry,' your ma said.

"I remember the old buzzard looking down at the meager food on our table like he'd won some prize. His face looked like a worn leather book. He was missing most of his teeth and had a scar across his right cheek. Looked more dead than alive."

Pa paused and sipped his coffee. "Somethin' came over me. Your ma asked me what I was doin' as I broke the last loaf of bread in half. 'I'm feedin' a hungry man,' I told her. She looked at me like I was crazy, but I just told her we were goin' to share what we had.

"You and Mary just stared wide-eyed at that old Indian in tattered buckskin. His moccasins were so frayed they barely held on his feet.

"I handed him the bread. He took it, grunted, then turned and walked out the door.

"The next morning, we heard another knock on the door. The old Indian was walking away as your ma opened it. On the ground was an earthen bowl of dried berries and a leather pouch stuffed with dried buffalo meat.

"For the rest of that cold first winter, we'd occasionally find deer legs, skinned rabbits, and odd items from that Indian. Looked like they came from settlers. I don't even want to speculate on how the old Indian had come to own 'em. But he probably kept us alive."

Pa rubbed his eyes as if the memory tired him.

Laura looked at her father with deep affection. "I vaguely remember it, Pa," she said. "In my dreams I see an old, haunted-looking face, reaching out for food. I'm hungry too, but then I'm eating and laughing with you."

Pa sighed. "Dreams are like books without numbered pages. They can get kind of jumbled up and take some figurin' out."

"What happened to that old Indian?"

Pa sighed. "After that first winter, didn't see him again for a long while. Our crops came in and we put away enough money to get by on."

Pa sipped his coffee. "But then came the government order to get out of the Indian Territory. You and Ma were in tears and Mary weren't sayin' nothin'. After I loaded the wagon, you made me open the back flap so you could say good-bye to that house you loved. I was pullin' away, tryin' to hold back tears myself, when I heard a wailin' from over by the creek trees.

"That old Indian was sittin' cross-legged, tossin' dust and pieces of whatever from his leather pouch into the air, wailin' like he was mournin' the dead.

"My hair stood on end. I gave him the once over eye, and that old buck gave me a smile and nodded his head, pointing his finger toward the sky. Never told anyone about that. Never."

CHAPTER 14

FEVER

Pa picked up his coffee cup and opened the back door. "Think I'll go out to the barn and wait for Manly. Lord, I wish blackberries were in season." He strolled across the yard toward the barn.

Blackberries. Laura took her cup of coffee and walked to the front porch, deep in thought. She sat in her favorite rocker, remembering those warm days in June, back on the prairie.

The Indians had gone, mounting their ponies to ride to the cooler high prairie, hunting for buffalo, so it was safe to play outside. Pa had told her that the Indians had to ride farther on their hunt each year and returned with fewer skins and robes because the white men were shooting so many buffalo for sport.

"The prairies are littered with wasted animals," he'd told her the morning she'd left to pick blackberries.

The creek bottoms where Laura went were thick with blackberries. The sun was so hot that Laura stayed in the shade, filling her bucket.

Blue jays pecked at her bonnet for taking their berries, and lazy deer lay in the damp creek bottom groves, watching little Laura. She was careful to watch for the snakes that seemed to be always underfoot and laughed at the squirrels who chattered overhead.

The creek bottoms were also thick with mosquitoes. Everywhere she went, they swarmed around her. Though the mosquitoes were fat from sucking on the sweet, ripe berry juice, they clamped on Laura's arms, face, and neck.

Every bite hurt, and the more Laura tried to slap them away, the more they swarmed around her. Her fingers were wet and purple from the berries, and soon her face and arms were stained a dark purple.

As the days grew hotter, the mosquitoes began swarming into their prairie home. Thick swarms of them settled into the rafters, under the eaves, and behind the beds. Pa tried burning damp grass around the house and stable, but the smudge smoke didn't keep the terrible pests away.

After a week, Laura's face and arms were a swollen mess. Pa could not play his fiddle, because he was swollen from the bites. The mosquitoes were everywhere, in everything. Every morning, Laura would awake to find her forehead thick with them, sucking through the skin on her forehead and nose.

"This can't last long," Pa had told them. "Fall's not too far away, and the first cold wind will get rid of 'em."

But the winds didn't come, and Laura began aching. She didn't feel like playing; she felt a chill into her soul. Not even the hot sunshine or a blazing fire could warm her.

This was the start of the fever and ague. It was one of the most common sicknesses on the prairie in America. It made you sleepy, cold, and weak, and it left its mark with thousands of graves throughout the frontier.

Her mother was concerned and asked, "Where do you ache, Laura?"

"I ache all over," Laura whispered from her bed. "My legs, my arms, my head. It all aches, Ma."

Laura lay there shivering as if it were forty below outside. Her teeth wouldn't stop chattering, though her skin was hot as fire.

They needed a doctor, but Pa and Mary were sick, too, and Ma couldn't leave them to go to the nearest town. But it was only a matter of days until Ma was sick and they were all lying on the floor of the cabin, moaning deliriously.

"Water . . . I'm thirsty, Ma," Laura whimpered. But her mother was too sick to help.

Mary was worse than Laura and looked like she was going to die. "Please, Laura, help me," Mary whimpered.

Jack the dog sat by her bed, moaning with fear. He went back and forth from Pa to Laura, not knowing what to do.

So Laura reached out for Jack the dog's collar. "Help me, boy," Laura whispered.

With the dog dragging her, Laura pulled herself along with her other hand. Though Laura heard jabbering fever voices in her brain, she concentrated on reaching the water pail in the corner.

She took the dipper and drank as much as she could hold, then held the dipper full of water in one hand and crawled back to her sister's bed. "Drink this, Mary," she whispered.

Falling back on the floor, Laura could remember feeling as if she had died. That the voices she was hearing in her brain were angels.

Then she looked up to the most beautiful smile she had ever seen in her life. A round, black face was looking down on her, and thick arms were picking her up.

"Who are . . . ?" she whispered to the glowing face.

"Drink this, little thing," he said softly.

As Laura sipped, she stared at the man's face. She had never seen a black man before.

"Who are . . . you?" she asked.

"I'm Dr. Tan, and you're a sick little girl."

Laura could not take her eyes off the kindly doctor. *A black man,* she thought to herself as she sipped what he was giving her. *I've seen a black man.*

"Laura, when's Manly goin' to get up?" Pa asked, waking her from her thoughts.

"Oh, Pa, I was just thinking back to when we had the fever and Dr. Tan came."

"Strangest thing, that black doctor walkin' in out of the blue, carryin' a medicine man's amulet. If it hadn't been for the doctor and that bitter quinine he made us swallow, we'd have all died for sure," Pa said.

"He was the first black man I'd ever seen, and he saved my life."

"He was, wasn't he? I'm just glad his timing was so good."

"But you told me he was an Indian doctor. Isn't that what you said?"

Pa nodded. "Told me 'fore he left that working with the Indians helped him be a doctor. Those people didn't worry about whether he was a good doctor or not 'cause of his color."

"I just wonder how Dr. Tan came to save us," she wondered. "It just seemed like one minute we were all dying and the next minute he was cradling my head, talking softly, and telling me I was going to live." She turned to Pa. "He was a complete stranger, who came miles out of his way to help some white strangers. How'd he know?"

Pa shrugged. "He said an old Indian told him to come."

"Why did that old Indian take such an interest in us?" she asked.

"Maybe he was sort of like our guardian angel." Pa sighed. "Just imagine, a red man tellin' a black man to come save some white people he'd never seen before in his life," he said, shaking his head.

Laura looked off across Apple Hill's orchards. "Prejudice is a terrible thing, isn't it Pa?"

Pa nodded. "That it is, Laurie. It's somethin' we've got to work at every day."

CHAPTER 15

ABC GUM

Rev. Youngun watched his children walk down the drive toward school. "Don't get in any trouble," he called after them.

"Oh, sure!" Beezer squawked from his perch in the parlor.

Uncle Cletus called out, "See you," and went back into the kitchen.

Dangit the dog struggled to get free from the rope. They'd tied him to the front porch rail because Miss O'Conner, their teacher from Ireland, was upset.

Good old Dangit kept sneaking into the school and hiding behind the coat rack. Every time some kid said "Dangit," Dangit rushed out and pulled at his pants cuffs.

As they turned the fence corner, Sherry skipped up to her brother. "Terry, do Pat-a-Cake with me, please?"

Terry shook his head and tossed a rock at a squirrel that was chattering at them from a branch overhead. "Fur-get-it!"

"Please," she begged. "Here's how it goes. Pat-a-cake, pat-a-cake, baker's man. So I will, master, as fast as I can. Pat it . . ."

Terry interrupted her. "Pat this," he said, swatting his rump, then hers.

Sherry jumped and cried out, "Larry. Larry! Terry hit me! Hit him! Hit him back!"

Larry tried to ignore their bickering. "Knock it off, you two. I'm tryin' to concentrate on my spellin' words."

He mumbled to himself, "Harass . . . h . . . a . . . r . . . ass."

Terry's eyes were wide. "Pa's goin' to get you for sayin' a dirty word."

"What?"

"You said the donkey word."

"I did not!" Larry exclaimed. "I was spellin' harass, not that other word."

Terry skipped around, trying to think about anything but school. "How come teachers can have substitutes? Why can't kids have substitutes? I'd give someone my lunch cookie every day if I could just stay home and play."

Larry ignored the question, but Terry continued. "What good's school, anyway? Teacher just asks dumb questions like 'Name things that are made of wood.' Everybody knows trees are made of wood." He paused and kicked a can, trying to get Larry's attention. He was still bothered by smarty-pants Li Sung Chan, son of Mr. Chan who owned the Chinese store and laundry in town.

"Course ol' brainhead Li had to go and say that George Washington's false teef were made of wood—who cares?" He kicked the can again. "I ain't never gonna eat with his ol' teef anyhow."

Terry popped a piece of bread into his mouth, watching Larry struggle to memorize the words, his tongue darting out as he silently sounded out the words on his list. Terry skipped along-side, already eating part of his lunch. "Want me to test you?" he asked. A piece of bread was hanging from his mouth.

"Don't talk with your mouth full!" Larry said, looking away in disgust. Then he turned back, shaking his head. "You can't hardly read. How you gonna test me?"

"I know the words," Terry said, full of confidence.

Larry smirked. "Oh yeah? Spell *Mississippi.*"

Terry wiggled around. "Mississippi . . . M . . . o . . . ss . . . oss . . . opp . . . i! Got it right, didn't I?" he beamed.

Larry shook his head in disgust. "That's moss-o-soup-e. I said Mississippi."

"Big deal!" Terry replied. "Bet I can beat you countin' to one hundred!"

Larry picked up a rock and tossed it. "Cannot. I'm almost three years older 'n you. That's three years more brains in my head."

"Can too beat you. Wanna bet?"

"What you gonna bet?" asked Larry, trying to figure out what angle his squirrely brother was going to take.

"Bet you my special hidden candy stash."

Terry's candy stash was his most cherished possession. He looked at it every night before he went to sleep, always nibbling on something. Larry knew that if Terry was willing to bet the stash, Terry meant business.

"Okay, you're on!" Larry shouted. "On your mark, get set, go!" Larry immediately started counting, "One . . . two . . . three . . . four . . ."

Terry didn't seem in any hurry, eating the rest of his sandwich and then taking out a piece of gum and chewing until it juiced. He even had time to scratch in several places and toss another rock, breaking a bottle by a fence.

When Larry was up to ninety-five, Terry suddenly screamed out, "One-two, skip-a-few, ninety-nine, one hundred!"

Larry stopped at ninety-six, red in the face from all his counting. "That's not fair! You cheated!"

Terry wiggled his rump at his brother and danced away. "You count your way and I'll count mine . . . sucker!"

Sherry skipped by them, saying her version of "Yankee Doodle." Larry stopped and listened. "Did you teach her that?"

"Yeah. Better than the one in the book, ain't it?"

Sherry skipped a figure eight and sang it a second time:

> Yankee Doodle drove to town,
> And almost hit a deer,
> Crashed into a big oak tree
> And landed on his rear

Sherry turned and beamed at Larry. "Terry taught me that. Said the teacher's goin' to like it!"

Larry shook his head. "You're gonna get her in trouble," he fretted, watching Sherry skip ahead of them.

"Any trouble she gets into, she deserves. Pa still calls her 'Baby Sherry.' Never heard of no almost-five-year-old baby 'fore."

Larry shrugged. "Calls her his 'last one,' whatever that means."

Making a face, Terry asked, "Who'd want another one like her, anyway?"

"What does monkey business mean?" asked Sherry.

"You don't know?" sneered Terry.

"I guess it means playing with monkeys," said Sherry. "I don't want to take care of no monkeys. They probably make a mess hangin' on the curtains.

The Younguns got to school before the bell, so they'd have

time to talk with their friends. Several of the boys were wearing stocking caps pulled way down over their ears.

"What's wrong with them?" Terry asked his brother.

"Must be cold or somethin'," Larry said, shaking his head.

"Someone ought to tell 'em they look like a bunch of woolly caterpillars."

Missouri Poole whistled to Larry from across the play area. She was tall, attractive, and an Okie to her roots. What bothered Larry was the pipe she smoked every day after school.

"Hey, sweetie. Remember, you're *my* valentine." She blew him a kiss and went back to tossing a football to the boys.

"Oh, man!" Terry said in a mocking tone. *"You got yourself a sweetie."*

"Not my choosin'," Larry said, shaking his head.

"With Missouri, she does the choosin' and you do the acceptin'," Terry chuckled.

Brooke Calahan, a dark-haired little cutie with eyes for Terry, skipped by and waved. "Hi, Terry."

"Get outta here!" Terry shouted, kicking the air behind her. "Don't need no girl makin' eyes at me!"

"Think she likes you," deadpanned Larry.

Terry kicked the dirt. "Don't care if she likes eatin' dirt—*I don't like girls.*"

"You're gettin' mad," Larry teased.

They walked to the edge of the playing field to watch Missouri pass the football. "That girl can throw," Larry mumbled.

Over on the side of the field, Zeke Wechter, the rag merchant's son, was studying his McGuffey reader.

"Look at him," Terry said, shaking his head. "Always studyin'."

Larry answered, "Zeke says he learned how to play the piano when he was just four years old."

"Don't believe that," Terry scoffed. "Heck, I was hardly potty-trained by four, so he wasn't playin' no piano."

Johnny Scales, son of the town's telegraph operator, hobbled by on a single crutch. Crippled since his first year by polio, Johnny was always in a good mood.

"Hi, guys," Johnny smiled.

Larry smiled. "One crutch? Thought you needed two?"

Johnny laughed. "Can't play football on two crutches. With one crutch I can almost catch the ball."

Larry shook his head, watching Johnny cross the field. "I feel sorry for him, you know?"

"Yeah," said Terry. "Say, how do you catch polo?"

"I think he's got polio. He caught it when he was a baby."

Terry scratched his head, watching Missouri lob a short pass to Johnny, which he missed, tripping on his crutch.

Larry whistled. "Nice try, Johnny!"

Terry shook his head. "I don't think football's gonna work for him."

"Hey, Terry," Sweettooth, the overweight son of the town's baker, cried out from the side of the backstop. "Got any more of that ABC gum?"

"Got any money?" Terry shouted back.

Chubbs held up a coin, and Terry motioned him over.

Larry pinched Terry's arm. "What's ABC gum? Gimme some!"

Terry took a piece of gum from his mouth and held it up. "You sure you want some of my *Already Been Chewed* gum?"

Before Larry could answer, Terry wrapped the gum in a piece of paper he had in his back pocket and pressed it flat. Sweet held out his penny. "What flavor is it today?"

Terry closed his eyes as if deep in thought, then opened one eye and looked at Sweet. "This is a new flavor. Called Wrigley's Bacon and Eggs."

Sweet pressed the penny into Terry's hand. "Gimme it, quick. I'm starvin'!" Terry took the penny, and Sweet tore the wrapper off the ABC and stuffed it into his mouth. "Tastes great! Thanks, Terry," he mumbled between chews.

Larry turned to his brother as Sweet walked away. "Bacon and Eggs? That's what we had for breakfast!"

"I know." Terry smiled, flipping his penny.

Larry showed his tongue in a gagging gesture. "Yuck!"

The school bell rang, and Terry raced ahead to take his seat. "Come on, let's go!" he shouted back.

Laura's column on head lice was pinned on the door of the school. Larry stopped to read it, but Terry kept bugging him.

"What's it say? What's it say?"

"Hush!" Larry said sternly. "Can't read with all your babbling."

"What's it 'bout?"

"'Bout cooties."

"Read it out loud. Please?" Terry asked.

"Yeah," said several other voices in unison. Larry turned around. A half-dozen of the smaller kids were gathered behind him.

"All right, but everyone listen up, 'cause I'm only goin' to read this once." He slowly read the article, stumbling on the bigger words.

WATCH OUT FOR HEAD LICE!

It seems that just about this time every year, a case or two of head lice breaks out in the county school. Dr. George wants to warn everyone that this is the time of year when the terrible critters try to invade the scalps of young and old alike.

I've gotten several letters from parents asking what they can do to protect their children. Well, the best prevention is to understand the problem.

Don't believe the old wives' tales or the gossip from the hills. Head lice don't jump or fly from head to head. They aren't part of a hex or curse.

They get from one head to another when you put on someone else's hat or earmuffs. That's why kids seem to get it so easily, because swapping clothes just seems to come natural to our young people.

Don't share a comb or use someone's brush! That's a head louse's favorite means of transportation. That's how it spreads through beauty parlors and by the terrible habit of men using the combs they find left in public bathrooms.

Warn your children and guard yourself from these practices, for it is not old wives' tales that spread the head lice. It is old habits!

Don't let your kids pile their stocking hats in the corner. Teachers and ministers should make a point of stopping this activity.

Parents, inspect your children's heads every day until the threat of head lice has once again left our area. Be on the lookout for those teeny, tiny, oval-shaped, silver-colored nits—the eggs of the head louse—which are only as big as the head of a sewing needle.

Don't be embarrassed to use a magnifying glass to inspect your young ones'—or old ones'—scalps. It's better to be embarrassed over something silly than to have your head shaved!

Martin Maggie—whom the kids called Martin Maggot—tugged at Larry's sleeve when he finished. Larry turned and frowned, because Maggot was always dirty and disheveled, and gave Larry the creeps just being near him.

"What do you want, Maggot?" Larry asked.

Maggot began scratching . . . and scratching . . . and scratching. "What are the signs of head lice again?" he asked.

The kids watching Maggot scratch soon began scratching themselves. Larry shuddered and walked away, saying, "Lice make you itch. Stay away from me, Maggot. I don't want your cooties."

The other kids jeered, and Martin Maggot was left by himself on the front steps, scratching his scalp.

"Wish someone would be my friend," he said with downcast eyes.

He saw Terry peering around the doorway. "Hey, Terry, would you be my buddy?"

"Forget it, Maggot! I'd rather hang out with a cockroach."

"Children, come in—school's starting," Miss O'Conner called out.

Martin Maggot walked dejectedly into the classroom, sitting by himself in the corner. Larry saw the tear in his eye and reached over and patted him on the head. "What's wrong, Maggot?"

"Terry won't be my friend."

"Can't force people to be friends," Larry whispered.

"But no one likes to play with me."

"'Cause you don't take baths. Clean yourself up right and you can play with everyone."

"Even football with you, Larry?"

"Maybe," Larry said.

No one noticed Dangit the dog slinking into the room. He

headed straight for the coat pile and crawled under, content to nibble on the lunches around him.

Miss O'Conner raised her hands for quiet. "We're goin' to have some visitors from the Monroe Street Parish School in St. Louis. They're coming by train tomorrow as part of a city–farm exchange program. These Monroe Street children have never been out of the city. They've never seen a farm, never seen a cow. Can you imagine that?"

"Don't they got cows in St. Louie?" asked Sweet.

Little James, Terry's black neighbor, raised his hand. "Everybody's seen a cow, ain't they?"

The teacher smiled. "That's what the program's all about. They're comin' here to see farm life, and then some of you lucky children will get to experience city life. They don't know where milk comes from, and you farm children probably don't know where it goes."

"Goes in your stomach," mumbled Terry.

Miss O'Conner heard him. "That's right. But before it gets to their stomachs in the city, it's got to be picked up, packaged, shipped, and delivered by the milkman."

"The who?" asked Missouri Poole.

"The milkman. In cities they have people who do nothing but deliver milk."

Little James smiled. "That's what I do every day after school."

"That'll be the day," mumbled Terry. "All you do is lick the cream from the buckets like a barn cat." He licked in the air like a cat and pointed to Little James.

Little James made a playful fist and swung an air punch. "I'll get you," he laughed.

"Children, children," Miss O'Conner continued, "you'll all get a chance to meet these children from the city and help introduce them to the country." She walked over and stood next to the Younguns. "I understand that Mr. Springer has asked Rev. Youngun's children to help show the Monroe Street Parish children around his farm." She patted Terry on the head. "And I know that you Younguns will be kind and show them how things really work on a farm."

Terry looked at Larry. They both got the same idea at the same time. "We'll be glad to," said Larry.

Terry smiled angelically. "You can trust us, Teacher."

"Sure," whispered Little James into Terry's ear.

Terry whipped around and made a fist.

"Boys! Boys," Miss O'Conner said, "I want you to use your best manners around our guests."

"Will they be here through Valentine's Day?" Sweet asked, worried that he'd have to share the school cupcakes with more kids.

"Maybe you'll all make new valentines," the teacher teased.

Missouri Poole hit Larry in the head with a rolled-up note. He pulled it open and read it silently. "You are *my* valentine." Turning as if his neck were rusted in place, Larry saw Missouri puckering her lips toward him, blowing air kisses. He turned quickly back around, blushing the color of a red apple.

Sweet waved to the teacher. "Dangit, that's not fair! I don't want to be sharin' the cupcakes with any more kids! Ain't 'nough as it is."

Dangit the dog perked up from the pile of coats in the corner when he heard his name misused. He came tearing across the floor and grabbed onto Sweet's pants cuffs, pulling him across the room.

"Hey! Hey, stop! Somebody get this dog off me!" he screamed.

Poochie tapped Terry. "I think that fool dog of yours is crazy, boy!"

Terry was smiling, watching Sweet being spun in circles. "I think ol' Dangit's just got a good sense of humor."

Dangit ripped the cuff of Sweet's pants; then he ripped off the whole pants leg, leaving Sweet standing there with his polka-dot underwear exposed!

Miss O'Conner tried to stop the bedlam, but Dangit ran through the room, shaking the pants leg around like a trophy.

"Go for the polka-dot undies!" Red shouted.

Finally, in desperation, Miss O'Conner called out to the Younguns, "Will one of you Younguns take your dog home?"

Terry jumped up. "I'll be glad to." Winking at Larry, he grabbed his book bag and whispered, "See ya later. Hope you enjoy the math."

"When you comin' back?" Larry whispered.

"Depends on how good the fishin' is," Terry laughed, racing toward the door.

"Let's go, Dangit," he scolded, dragging the dog from the room. "I told you, *just bite girls.*"

"Come back as fast as you can," Miss O'Conner called after him.

"You can trust me," Terry laughed, jumping two stairs at a time and heading toward the creek.

CHAPTER 16

JOHNNY

Johnny Scales watched Terry run off down the road. *Wish I could run like that,* he thought. *Wish I could run just once.*

Growing up with polio had not been easy. It was a mystery disease that no one had an answer for. Though his parents thought he was sleeping when the doctor had come to the house, he could remember those words from years ago as if it were yesterday.

"He'll never walk normally again," the doctor had told his father.

"Never?" his father asked.

"Johnny will be on crutches for the rest of his life."

Johnny knew that his father had taken it the worst. *I was to be his pride and joy,* Johnny thought. *I was to follow in his footsteps.*

Football, he thought. *That's a game that takes two good legs. No one wants a cripple on their team.*

Johnny looked over at Larry Youngun, envious of his handsome face and strong body. But he couldn't begrudge Larry what he was born with. Just like he couldn't change what had happened to him.

The only time he'd ever played football was when Larry put him on the Younguns' team. Though Johnny knew that Larry was just being kind, it was still special.

Just being on the field was special to Johnny. Football was such a rough-and-tumble sport, but it was something boys loved. *Something that boys who could run and jump did,* he thought.

Johnny had learned to hobble on one crutch so he could have a free hand to catch the ball. Missouri Poole had even played catch with him. Though he caught it several times, they were still easy passes. *Thrown by a girl,* he frowned.

I know she's just bein' nice, he thought, looking over at the tall girl. She was so pretty that it made Johnny nervous. *I wish I had a girlfriend like her. But she likes Larry,* he thought. *No girl will ever like me.*

If only I could play football, he thought. *Then I could show everyone what I'm really made of.*

While the teacher read to the class about the founding of America, Johnny's mind was somewhere else. He was in a world of his own. A world where he could run and jump . . . and play football.

It was the big moment of the game and everyone was hushed. It was all on Johnny's shoulders. Dashing down the field, he turned to see the quarterback throw a high spiral down the field.

Johnny ran his heart out, his fingers outstretched to catch the ball. *I can do it, I can do it,* he thought, his heart pounding.

The crowd in the bleachers was cheering. *I know I can catch it, I know it!*

"Johnny, Johnny . . . I'm speaking to you."

Johnny blushed, snapping out of his daydream. The children were giggling.

"Johnny, I asked if you knew what the Bill of Rights is about."

"Football," Johnny mumbled, without thinking.

CHAPTER 17

FREDDIE'S SONG

While Pa and Manly walked and talked around Apple Hill Farm, Laura took the time to read her column in the *Mansfield Monitor*. Andrew Jackson Summers, her editor, always had a copy of the paper delivered on the days her column was featured.

Satisfied with the article, she straightened up the house, dusted the furniture, swept the kitchen, and shooed old dog Jack out onto the porch.

She thought about Pa's Indian story and wondered what other strange and wondrous tales lay in the back of his mind. Maybe a short ride with him *would* do her a world of good.

They could take her Oldsmobile, pack a picnic lunch, and ride around the countryside, talking about the old days. Of course, Pa's idea was to try and be a pioneer again, but Laura knew that was just foolish talk. *Who ever heard of two grown people just taking off like that?* she thought.

Then she stopped in front of the hall mirror and faced herself. Pa had been her age when he'd headed off into Indian Territory. He'd had all his adventures when he was older than she was now. Why was she too old to go?

She had washed Pa's train clothes and dried them on the

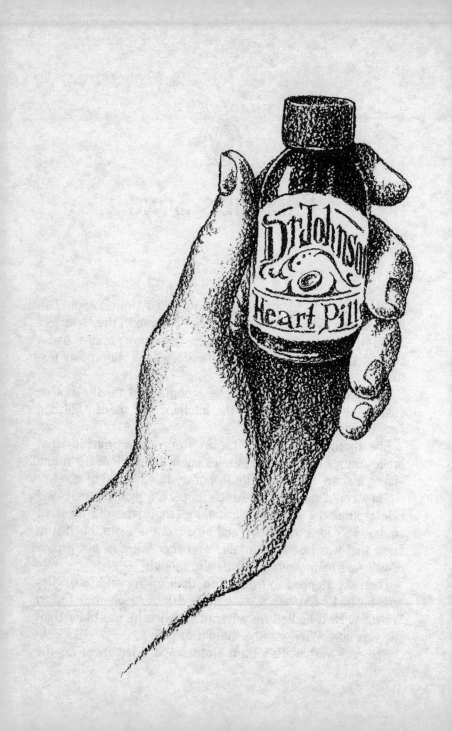

porch rail. As she folded them, she waved to Pa and Manly, who were walking the cows to the back pasture.

Carrying his clothes to his room, Laura smiled at the way Pa had arranged his simple items on the dresser top. He'd never had much and never seemed to want much. He always gave away everything he got to help others.

Laura shook her head, remembering how Pa had used their entire savings to buy the church a bell and the time he nearly cleaned out their pantry to feed a poor family down the road.

Opening a drawer, Laura placed the shirt and pants neatly on top of his other folded clothes. She smoothed the wrinkles out of the shirt and felt a lump underneath. Feeling around under the bottom shirt, she pulled out a pill bottle. The label said, "Dr. Johnson's Heart Pills."

"Heart pills," she whispered, remembering the way he had held his chest in pain. She didn't hear Pa coming up the stairs. He stopped at the doorway and saw what she was holding, so he cleared his throat.

Laura turned, red with embarrassment. "Pa, I was just . . . I'm . . . I'm sorry, Pa."

He sighed, shaking his head. "You got a right to know. Doc said I got heart problems and gave me them pills." Taking a deep breath, he continued. "Been havin' pains. Guess you know that."

"Are you going to be okay, Pa?"

"Doc said they might get worse, and they are doin' that," he said with a grin. "Can't stop gettin' old, but I sure wish it didn't have to be painful."

Laura took his arm. "Sit down and rest, Pa."

He shook her off. "Daggonit, Laurie, quit it! I ain't ready for no old folks' home—at least not yet—not 'til I see our prairie homestead one last time."

"You really think you should be making any kind of trip at all, Pa?"

"Yes and no. Yes, I wanna, and no, I probably shouldn't." He began coughing, grabbing onto the dresser for support. Laura looked worried and put her arm around him. When the coughing subsided, he continued. "I want to see it again. Might be my last time to try—my last trip. Will you come with me?"

Laura looked into his eyes, then wrapped her arms around him, trying to remember her father as the young man he once was, standing on the wagon bed, challenging the world. "Yes," she whispered, "I'll go with you, Pa."

Pa closed his eyes. "Thank you." He looked at Laura and lifted her head up. "Smile, my little half-pint of sweet cider half drunk up!"

When Laura saw his smile, her worries melted away. "I'll try."

"Try? We're goin' *home*. We're goin' home to the prairie!"

After Laura told Manly about her decision, they argued all day. He said, "It's a foolish idea, woman your age, traipsing round the countryside with an old man, lookin' for somethin' that you know ain't there."

Laura knew in her heart that the whole idea was crazy, but she was driven by her spirit of adventure and the desire to please her father. "It'll just take a day or two. We'll take the good road to Springfield, then through Joplin to Independence, then into Kansas and . . ."

Manly interrupted her, shaking his head. "And you'll be lucky if the car makes it to Springfield, the way the roads are. Who's gonna fix the car or change a tire? *You?*"

Laura shrugged. "We'll just find a livery or a blacksmith to help us if we need it."

"You'll be stuck who-knows-where, at the mercy of some

blackhearted blacksmith takin' advantage of you bein' a woman and your pa bein' an old man."

Pa had come up behind them on the porch, carrying his violin. He listened to the last part of the conversation and startled them when he spoke. "I can take care of us if somethin' happens. Always have and always will."

Manly pushed aside his embarrassment at being overheard and looked directly at Pa. "I admire what you did in crossin' the prairie years ago, but times have changed. You don't know nothin' about motor cars or fixin' 'em."

Pa put his violin down and shrugged good-naturedly. "We'll be all right."

Laura nodded. "That's right! Just have a little faith, Manly."

Manly looked at them both, measuring his words very carefully. "I believe that you both are makin' a mistake. My advice is, *don't go.*"

In frustration he turned away for a moment, then turned to look at Laura. "I've never been one to convince you to do somethin' once you've got your mind set otherwise. If you don't want my advice, then you don't want my advice."

He walked toward the porch door, but Laura grabbed his arm. "Please, don't be mad."

Shaking off her arm, Manly opened the door. "I'm mad now, and I'll be worried sick if you go—but you two *pioneers* don't seem to want my advice."

"Maybe he's right," Laura said, lost in thought.

Pa started to pick up his violin, then stood and put his arm around her shoulders. "And maybe he's wrong—which he is. Now you better get packin'. I'll be ready to go in the mornin'."

"It won't take me long. We're just going to be gone a few days."

Pa clicked his tongue. "Few days? Fiddlesticks! We may like

ridin' in a wagon on the prairie so much that we'll never come back. Just ride off into the sunset."

"Wagon?" she frowned. "We're not taking our farm wagon. We're going to take the Oldsmobile, so we can get there and back."

Pa snorted. "Ain't never heard of a pioneer of the prairie travelin' by motor car. We'll look like tourists out for a Sunday picnic. We're takin' the wagon, and that's all there is to it!" he said, crossing his arms.

"We are not!"

"Are too," he said sternly, looking at her through one closed eye. "It's the wagon or I'm not goin'!"

Laura went to the door and opened it. "Then I'll go by myself! You're the one who came up with this crazy idea, and now my husband's all upset with me."

Pa softened. "But, Laurie, it won't be the same travelin' in a motor car like pantywaists."

Stamping her foot, Laura gritted her teeth in frustration. "If you want to come, then you better get your panties ready, cause this pantywaist is leavin' at sunup—with or without you." She closed her eyes and breathed deeply, then slammed the door behind her, saying, "Men!"

Pa looked out toward the sunset and grumbled, "Women!"

An early grasshopper flew onto the porch rail, scratching his legs. Pa flicked him off. "Get out of here! Go on back to Egypt."

Though the Ozark sunset was beautiful, the grasshopper brought back the terrible memory of a dark cloud on the horizon—a dark, heaving, chattering mass of destruction that changed Pa's life forever.

Though they had to leave their home in Indian Territory, he had made the best of the trip, singing and playing his violin as they crossed the seemingly endless prairie in search of a new home.

They went for days not seeing another living soul, just a man and a woman and their three daughters, alone against the world.

"I'm gonna build you another house, Caroline!" he shouted out to the world. "It'll be the best place we ever had." Ma sat there smiling, nodding to him as always, accepting the fate dealt to them.

He had promised her so many things and only asked one thing in return. "When we build our new house, I want to have a son."

"Oh, Charles," Ma said, "we've already got three children."

"Just one more, Caroline. I want to have a son. Gonna name him Frederick Charles Ingalls. He'll inherit everything we build from this point on."

He found another place on the prairie with land so fertile that everything seemed to grow, and soon they had a wheat crop so deep and thick that even Ma was caught up in Pa's enthusiasm for the future.

The whole family marveled at the beauty of the crop each evening at sunset. Ma talked about the new things she'd buy for the house, and the children talked of store-bought toys.

They had planned to bring in the harvest during the first week of August. The weather had been perfect, with just enough rain to give the stalks an extra two inches of growth.

On the last day of July, Pa had gone into town to pick up some supplies. At the feed store, a few of the men had gathered around Old Lady Winny, known throughout the area as an expert in Bible searching.

Bible searching had come to America with the Pilgrims, who used it to guide their actions. Like picking a card or consulting a fortune teller, misguided religious believers consulted Bible searchers, who would flip through the pages of the Bible and stop and point to a passage.

What the passage was about was what the future held in store for the person having the search done. Farmers on the prairie always asked searchers to see what was in store for them before the harvests came. Would they get enough rain or would the frost come early. Though it was a mixing of the Bible with seers and fortune telling, prairie ministers mostly ignored it.

Old Lady Winny, her toothless smile lost in a sea of weathered wrinkles, had her Bible in hand. The farmers were tossing her coins, asking for a Bible search.

"Come on Winny, tell us what's comin' up," an Irish farmer called out, tossing her a penny.

"Yeah, tell us how rich we're all gonna be," a big strapping farm lad laughed.

"What kind of price are we gonna get for our wheat?" a big strapping farm lad asked.

Pa edged closer to listen in. He started to flip his lucky gold piece, then for some reason put it back into his pocket. Something told him that this wasn't the time or place to push his luck.

Old Lady Winny touched the faces of the men, speaking in tongues, looking for the spirit. She scratched on one, tapped on another, and pulled on the cheek of the big farm boy.

When she got to Pa, Old Lady Winny paused, letting her gnarled fingers creep across his cheeks. An odd, cold, tingling sensation made him shiver.

Then she raised her hand into the air. A few of the men nervously grinned at each other, pushing forward for a closer look. She dropped her hand, and the men fell back. Her pupils had disappeared, leaving only the ghostly, haunting whites of her eyes.

Pa wanted to step back, but stood his ground, strangely fascinated by this old woman. It was like a rock he shouldn't turn over, a secret better not to know, or a page he was told not to read.

Old Lady Winny began softly speaking in a strange language, spittle flying from her lips as she talked louder and louder. Her fingers flipped through the book, turning the pages faster and faster.

Though the day was warm, a chill went through the men. They felt the hair on their necks rising as her garbled speech got louder and louder. Then she began moving her head up and down, calling out, *"No!"* between her foreign sentences.

A farmer named Norm Stevenson muttered loud enough for everyone to hear, "What's wrong? What's she doin'?"

Pa felt a wave of cold come over him, as if something was telling him to close his eyes, not to hear what she was going to say.

Then she started shaking up and down, screaming, *"No!"* as if she was trying to stop something from happening. Pa knew that something terrible was coming.

He wanted to leave—he started to leave. But she caught him by the sleeve, staring at him with her vacant eyes, shouting, *"No! No! No!"*

Pa tried to shake her off, but she clung to him with strength far beyond her size. One of the men tripped off the sidewalk and ran down the street with fear in his eyes.

Winny spun around, falling against the men, who reacted as if she were on fire. When her pupils came back, she was pointing to the book of Exodus.

"What—what's it say?" the old Irishman whispered, leaning forward, trying to figure out where her fingers had stopped.

But Old Lady Winny was in a world of her own and began reciting, "Behold, to morrow will I bring the locusts into thy coast: and they shall cover the face of the earth, that one cannot be able to see the earth . . ."

"Shut her up!" the Irishman screamed. "She's putting a curse on us." He reached out and grabbed her arm, but Winny shook it off.

Her crackling voice was building again with intensity. "The land was darkened; and they did eat every herb of the land, and all the fruit of the trees . . . there remained not any green thing in the trees, or in the herbs of the field . . ."

Some of the men backed away, holding their ears, as if to erase what she'd said. But Old Lady Winny kept reading, louder and louder until she reached the end.

Then, just as suddenly as it started, she stopped, out of breath and fearful of what she had found. Snapping her Bible shut, she picked up the coins the men had dropped at her feet and put them into her ancient purse.

Stevenson was the most upset, grabbing onto the arms of the men around him. "She's a witch! She's just a gypsy witch tellin' lies to get our money!"

He picked up a stick and held it in front of him as if to ward off some evil. "Go on . . . get on your broom, witch, and fly out of here!"

Old Lady Winny brushed by Pa, looking into his eyes, nodding with a solemn wink of her crinkled eye. He shivered with chills and did his business in town, hurrying home, trying to forget about what he'd heard.

On August first, while he and Caroline were out looking at

the best wheat crop they'd ever had, he saw a dark funnel cloud coming toward them.

"Is it a twister, Charles?" Caroline asked.

He looked, but wasn't sure. They hurried to gather up the children and rushed back to the house. The dark cloud was a chattering, throbbing mass of ravenous creatures. Old Lady Winny had predicted a plague of locusts, but this was far worse.

Before they could get inside the house, the creatures began to land on their shoulders and in their hair, to crawl across their lips. The nibbling, gnawing things were everywhere. Each step, each jump was onto a thick, living carpet, squishing beneath them.

Grasshoppers. Millions of chattering grasshoppers eating everything they landed on, had descended upon the prairie as far as the eye could see. He picked Carrie up under one arm and took Laura's hand. Caroline pulled Mary along, screaming as if the creatures were eating her alive.

When they reached the house, the front door was partially opened. Inside, on their beds, in their cups, and eating their food and curtains, was a solid green mass of destruction. They grabbed brooms to swat them from the house, but for every one they killed, a hundred more appeared. Little Laura screamed that the bugs were eating her dress, but Pa was too busy closing the windows.

By the time he'd gotten the house secured, Caroline's swatting had left a bloody, sticky mess all over the floors and walls. "We stopped 'em, Charles—we stopped 'em," she said.

Charles sighed for a moment, then heard a sound from the chimney. Before he could close the flue, a thick horde of grasshoppers slithered down the chimney. He stuck his hands up and pulled at the flue, trying to blow and spit off the grasshoppers covering his face.

Caroline swatted around him, trying to kill them before they could go farther. Laura and Mary stomped as many as they could with their feet, but Mary stopped in panic, screaming as her face and legs were covered with the green, sticky creatures.

The next morning, he opened the door and looked out on nothing but a carpet of grasshoppers. They'd eaten every leaf, every sprout. They'd eaten the entire wheat crop down to the ground. It was as if there were nothing left on earth but grasshoppers. And there was nothing left of his dream. The wheat was gone. The garden was gone. They had bills to pay and nothing to pay them with. The wheat crop that was going to set them free was gone. Caroline told him they could plant again, but he knew that was another false dream.

The grasshoppers had laid their eggs in the soil for hundreds of miles around, leaving billions of little land mines, waiting for the chance to ravage another crop. Neighbors committed suicide. Hundreds of prairie folks moved back east, trying to escape the locust that kept returning. The nation was facing a food disaster because the locust had eaten enough food to feed the entire nation. The President issued a national plea that everyone—every man, woman, and child—join with him in a week of prayer, asking for deliverance from this plague.

Then a miracle happened. The grasshoppers just seemed to vanish! Hallelujahs rang out on ten thousand church bells across the prairies.

But the grasshoppers had killed Pa's dream of being a prosperous farmer. To survive, he hitched rides on rails and marched for days with the other ragtag down-and-outs, trying to survive. He worked other people's farms, bringing back what money he could.

No matter how much money he made, it was never enough to keep his farm going and pay the taxes. Even though his first son, Frederick Charles—Freddie—had been born, there was no fiddle playing in the Ingalls household. Pa's fiddle stayed locked in its case. He had four children whose haunting, hungry eyes kept him awake every night.

Soon they were forced to leave the prairie for good. He paid the taxes and sold the house to pay off his debts, then loaded their wagon once again, this time heading east instead of west.

Freddie was almost nine months old, but he'd never heard his father's violin. Laura begged him to play, to sing a song like the old days, but he just shook his head. "I'm gonna wait until things turn around; then I'll play Freddie a special song, one just for him."

He picked up the gurgling baby boy and shook his head. "Times are bad now, but one day it'll have to get better. Then I'll play a song for you, son. I'll call it Freddie's Song."

"Play it for him now, Pa, please," Laura begged.

"No, Laurie. I've written it in my mind, but I won't put it to the fiddle until the time is right. Then Freddie will have his song."

But baby Freddie would never get to hear his song. A month later, Freddie died. Born during the plague and the bad times, baby Freddie had never heard Pa's violin.

Pa sagged against the rail on Laura's porch. He looked toward the heavens, eyes welling up, and whispered, "I'm sorry, Freddie. I should have played you your song."

Letting that little baby boy die without playing him a violin song from his heart was what haunted Pa. It grabbed him every time he picked up his violin, knowing how much the simple gift of love and music can mean.

Standing on the front porch of Apple Hill Farm, thinking about the terrible times, the plague, the lost crops, and the lost dreams, brought tears to Pa's eyes. He tried to hold them back, but they poured from him like a torrent.

Laura had paused in the doorway, about to say something, but held back, letting him cry his heart out for all the hurts he'd suffered.

Pa sniffed deeply, then picked up his violin from the open case and dug deeply with the bow, drawing out the first note. "Here's one for you, Freddie. Here's 'Freddie's Song.' "

Laura remembered burying her tiny baby brother back along the river, so long ago. Tears streamed down her face. "He's playing for you, Freddie," she whispered.

Manly came up, putting his arm around Laura. He said softly, "I don't understand, but then I do. You and your pa go and find that house of yours. Find what you've both been looking for."

CHAPTER 18

THE MONROE STREET TIGERS

"Choo-choo . . . choo-choo."

Richie Row looked at little Burpo Bennelli and covered his ears. Burpo had eaten another can of sardines and was smelling up the whole car. With that added to the constant train sounds he'd made since they left St. Louis, Richie was at wit's end. "Burpo, can't you say somethin' else?" Richie pleaded.

Burpo stopped halfway down the aisle of the train car and looked at Richie defiantly. "I like makin' train sounds. Choo-choo . . . choo-choo."

Then, without any warning, Burpo accidentally burped in Richie's face. Eyes watering, Richie pushed him away, screaming, "Quit eatin' those sardines! Your breath's enough to raise the dead!"

The St. Louis to Mansfield train ride had been anything but quiet for those unlucky enough to be stuck in car six. Nine children of the St. Louis Monroe Street Parish were on their way to experience country life.

Most of the Monroe Street Parish kids had never even been outside the city limits, and none had milked a cow or gathered eggs from a chicken house. If the trip was successful, rural children would be sent to St. Louis to see what city life was all about.

Four of the kids on the train were known as the Monroe Street Tigers, kids who hung together for protection and friendship. They adopted their name after helping catch an escaped circus tiger cub.

Through thick and thin, they had stuck together and promised to remain friends for the rest of their lives. They'd sealed the pact in blood, rubbing their pinpricked fingers together in the basement of the parish hall.

The leader of the Monroe Street Tigers was Richie Row, a twelve-year-old redhead with a face full of freckles. His mother was a Christian Scientist and his father a drinker. Neither of his parents had time for the other and neither had time for Richie, who was caught in the chaos of a marriage going bad, being pulled both ways without any real direction.

Father O'Reilly, head of the Monroe Street Parish, had seen him hanging around, watching the kids play basketball and football, so he invited him to play. "I'm not a Catholic," Richie had stated.

Father O'Reilly had laughed. "If you want to play, I'm inviting you into the game."

Geno "Burpo" Bennelli was the smallest of the Monroe Street Tigers. Seven years old and small for his age, Burpo loved three things: football, skipping school, and eating sardines—any kind of sardines. Big, little, with garlic, mustard, or plain, Burpo loved sardines. The kids had nicknamed him Burpo because he always burped after he ate the smelly fish— and it was terrible. He was the one player that nobody wanted to tackle after lunch.

Burpo's mother and father had left him with his grandparents to go back to Italy for a visit. That had been six years ago. They'd never been heard from again.

His grandparents had done the best they could with their limited means. His grandpa still did part-time butcher work when he could find it and took some of his pay in food—cases of sardines.

Mickey McGurk was eight, shy, and fat. He loved candy. His dad ran the McGurk Sweet Shop south of Monroe Street, and Mickey McGurk—whom the kids called Rollo—loved to work there after school.

No one knew why he was shy since his parents were very outgoing. But Rollo got nervous around people he didn't know. Richie and Burpo could always tell when one of his candy-anxiety attacks was coming on because he'd blush, sweat, and begin to wring his hands.

The only thing that would calm him down was candy—hard, soft, chewy, sweet, or sour. Since Rollo was nervous most of the time, he just got fatter and fatter.

The fourth Monroe Street Tiger was really a tigress—Annabell Davenport. Eleven years old, tall for her age, and exceptionally pretty, she and Richie shared the same misery of a home life going from bad to worse.

Annabell was a tough Tiger who hung with the three boys because they didn't call her names or allow people to tease her about her mother's wild ways. That's how she and Richie had become friends. He'd heard some of the parish boys tease Annabell.

Richie asked the boys to stop it and, when they teased her again, he knocked the biggest one to the ground and made him apologize.

So they called themselves the Monroe Street Tigers and hung together for more reasons than they understood. Their mascot was a stray mixed female chow they'd found behind the church. They took turns feeding her, sneaking her in and out of their homes.

They'd nicknamed the dog Chew-Chew for her bad habit of chewing on anything and everything. Father O'Reilly had told the kids not to bring the dog on the train, but who was going to feed her?

So Burpo wrapped her into his bedroll, and he and Rollo carried her right on board. Every time the conductor came round, they hid Chew-Chew under the seat.

The last time he'd come by, Chew-Chew had sniffed the shoes of the man sleeping soundly in the seat behind her. Richie thought the dog was sleeping, though he couldn't figure out how anyone could sleep with Burpo running up and down the aisle, shouting out, "Choo-choo," like the train.

Every time Burpo called out "choo-choo," Chew-Chew raised her head, thinking her name was being called. This time when Burpo went racing by, imitating a train, Chew-Chew raised her head at the same time the sleeping man moved his feet.

The man was wearing the best pair of Made in Missouri Brown's shoes and a banker's suit, vest, gold watch fob, and stiff-starched collar.

Burpo's train voice woke him up: "Choo-choo . . . choo-choo."

He rubbed his eyes and shouted with a snarl, "Hey, shrimp, shut your yap! I'm sick of hearin' you mouth off."

"Sorry, mister," Burpo whispered.

The man waved Burpo away, grumbling, "Your breath's worse than a fish market."

Burpo looked down and noticed that Chew-Chew had been working on the man's right shoe. He wiggled his finger for

Chew-Chew to come, but the dog just wagged her tail, licking the bottom of the man's shoe.

Burpo slipped into the seat in front of the man and looked under his seat. "Here, Chew-Chew. Come here, girl. Please, Chewy—you're gonna get us in trouble."

Chew-Chew wagged her tail but didn't move.

"Now, Chew-chew . . . come out now," Burpo said a little louder.

The man looked at Burpo's head going up and down and sighed. "Hope you're not gettin' sick kid. This car already smells like either a doghouse or dead fish."

With a sigh, the man wiggled around on the seat to get more comfortable. In the process, he moved his feet.

Chew-Chew growled softly. She had almost pulled off the sole of the man's shoe and didn't want to stop, so she bit down on it, moving it back into place.

The man look down, opening his mouth in astonishment. "Hey, you chewed up my shoe!"

He stood up, waving his arms, trying to get into the aisle, but Chew-Chew wouldn't let go. They pulled back and forth until the leather sole came off in one loud rip, sending the man backward onto the aisle floor.

Chew-Chew walked out into the aisle, thinking the man was playing with her. She wagged her tail, shaking the leather sole in her mouth.

Richie saw trouble brewing, so he nodded to Annabell, who diverted the man's attention. "Are you all right, mister?" she asked.

Richie scooped up the dog and did a pass-and-switch with Rollo, who put the dog in his big cloth traveling case.

"Where's that dog? Who owns that dog? Someone's gonna pay for my shoes!" shouted the man.

The conductor came into the car, shouting, "Mansfield, next stop. Five-minute rest stop."

With the man still screaming about a dog, it was all the conductor could do to restore order. He pushed the kids away and dusted the man's coat off.

"A dog chewed up my shoe!" the man exclaimed, pointing to his shoe.

"A dog, sir?" said the conductor with raised eyebrows, looking at the hole in the end of the man's sock. "I don't remember checking any dog onto this train."

"Are you callin' me a liar?" the man asked loudly.

"No, sir," the conductor said as politely as he could. "If you could just show me the dog, I'll be happy to handle this."

"The dog's right under here," the man said, pointing under the seat in front of his own. "He was hiding under—" His jaw dropped. "Where's the dog?"

With a wink and a quick gesture, the conductor pointed to the back of the car. "Step over here, sir, so we can discuss this quietly."

He took the man by the sleeve and pushed him along. After a few moments of heated discussion, the conductor came back. "Okay, you kids, where's the dog?"

"Dog, sir?" Burpo shrugged, raising his palms into the air. "There's no dog on the train, sir."

The conductor waved him silent. "If there ain't no dog, who chewed up this gentleman's shoe?"

The man had his shoe off and was looking through it at Burpo, who just shrugged. "Maybe he did it himself."

"I'm gonna whip your behind right here and now!" He stepped toward Burpo with his hand raised in the air.

Chew-Chew could sense what was happening and began

growling. The conductor spun around. "I hear it! Where's the dog?"

The Monroe Street Tigers were known for sticking together and taking a hand-off to keep the ball rolling, so Rollo grabbed his stomach, pretending to have a stomachache. "Oh-h-h, my stomach, it hur-r-r-rts," he moaned.

"There ain't no dog here," Burpo shouted. "That man just don't like kids!"

The man raised his hand again, and Richie stepped between them, counting the seconds until they got to Mansfield. "Please don't let 'em hurt us. We're orphans on our way to the orphan house."

"Orphans?" the conductor said. He turned to the man. "You're threatenin' to hit orphans?"

The man stammered, "I . . . I . . . my shoe . . . who's gonna pay for my shoe?"

Annabell began to cry. "We don't have any money."

"Yeah, we're starvin'!" Rollo moaned, rubbing his stomach.

The conductor looked at Rollo's face. "You don't look like you're starvin'."

The train whistle announced the upcoming stop. The conductor shouted out, "Mansfield, next stop. Make sure to check the seat for your belongings."

Rollo sat back down, made sure no one was watching, and opened his cloth suitcase. Chew-Chew looked up at him, wagging her tail.

"Give it to me, Chewy," Rollo whispered. "Give me the man's piece of shoe back."

"I'm missing a piece of my shoe!" the man said, his face getting redder by the moment.

"Here it is," said Rollo, holding out the man's shoe leather. The man grabbed it and started forward, "Why, you—I'm gonna . . ." The train lurched as it came around the turn, sending the man sprawling on top of Rollo, who fell on top of the suitcase. Chew-Chew was growling loudly, Rollo was pretending it was coming from his stomach, and the shoeless man was flailing his arms around like a baby bird.

The conductor lost his balance, knocking Burpo onto the man's chest. "Get off me, kid," the man shouted from the pileup.

Burpo struggled to get off him, but every time he was almost off, the train lurched again, sending them all back down again between the seats. Richie tried to pull Burpo off, but he saw the sheepish grin on Burpo's face and shook his head. "No, Burpo . . . not a—"

Burpo just shrugged and nodded. Then he got red in the face, puffed up his cheeks, and belched out some of the worst breath this side of an open-air fish market.

The man stopped his flailing and crossed his eyes, gasping for breath. "I'm dyin'!" he gagged. "Get this kid off me! He stinks like a dead fish. Help!"

Chew-Chew sprang from the cloth suit case and licked the man's face. The train whistled again and began slowing down.

The conductor picked up his hat. "Mansfield, all off who's gettin' off." Then he saw Chew-Chew. "Who owns that dog?"

"Never seen it before in my life," Burpo said, raising his shoulders and quickly crossing himself for the white lie.

Looking to Richie, the conductor said, "I want that dog off at Mansfield, you understand?"

"No problem. I'll take her off myself," Richie smiled.

The conductor walked past the shoeless man, who was sitting in the middle of the aisle. "What about my shoe?" the man called out.

"Find a one-legged man and split the cost of another pair,"

the conductor said, straightening out his coat as he walked toward the next car.

As the train approached the outskirts of Mansfield, Rollo looked out and saw a cow. "What's that?"

Annabell shook her head. "I think it's a sheep or somethin'."

"Naw," said Burpo, "sheep ain't that big. I bet it's a goat."

Annabell squiggled her nose. "Chew some gum or something, Burpo."

Richie laughed. "Don't you guys know a mule when you see one?"

The train came to a complete stop with a burst of smoke and cinders. Richie picked up Annabell's bag. "Come on, let's go out and teach these hicks a thing or two."

"Yeah, we're the Monroe Street Tigers," shouted Burpo.

"Think they play football?" asked Pudgie, looking out at the small town.

"Naw," chuckled Richie. "Be surprised if they can even tie their shoes. We'll be leadin' 'em round by the nose within a day or two!"

Across the platform, waiting for the train to Cape Girardeau, the Younguns were trying to convince their pa not to leave.

Annabell noticed Larry Youngun immediately, and when he caught her glance, they both blushed. "What a valentine he is," she whispered to herself.

"What're you lookin' at?" Richie asked, looking around to see what had attracted her attention. He saw the Younguns and laughed. "Look at those *hayseeds*. Man-oh-man, can you imagine livin' in this place?"

Rollo looked around and saw Larry frowning at the hayseed comment. "Bet they don't even have a decent bakery 'round here."

Burpo opened his bag and looked at his last can of sardines. "Let me know if you see a store. I need some more sardines."

"The way you smell, somebody's gonna put a fishhook in your mouth," Rollo laughed.

Annabell smiled at Larry, and when Richie wasn't looking, she winked at Larry, blowing him a kiss. Larry blushed again.

Then Father Walsh came up, his arms spread wide. "Children, children, welcome to Mansfield. I know you're as excited as I am about seeing how we live!"

"Yeah," Burpo whispered to Rollo, "whoop-de-do!"

"Do they play football?" Richie asked.

Father Walsh laughed. "They try, but maybe you'll have to teach them how the fighting Irish play the game! Did you bring a football with you?"

Richie nodded. "Show 'em, Rollo."

Rollo walked over behind the baggage cart and dragged over a large trunk on wheels. He undid the lock, lifted up the snap hinges, and threw open the lid. The trunk was filled with matching jerseys, pants, special shoes, leather helmets, and footballs."

"Now *that's* what I call ready to play football," Father Walsh beamed. "Now, let's get our bags together and go to the rectory for dinner."

Annabell saw Larry looking at her from the corner of his eye. She winked and giggled at Larry's blush. "Think we'll get a football game up with the local boys?" she asked Richie.

"Don't be thinkin' 'bout playin' games with any boys around here," Richie said with a frown. "I'll beat the livin' daylights out of anyone who gets around you!"

"I'll let you know who I don't want around." She frowned, looking over his shoulder at Larry.

"Come on, boys and girls," Father Walsh called out, waving his hands. "There's still time for evening mass before dinner."

On the other side of the platform, Rev. Youngun had Terry hanging on his leg and Sherry tugging on his arm.

Larry had been holding onto his other arm, but dropped it when the train arrived—when the pretty girl arrived. Even though the guy had called them hayseeds, all Larry could think about was that girl.

Rev. Youngun waved his arms in desperation. "Children, children, I have to go. I'll only be in Cape Girardeau a few days."

"Don't go. Please, Pa," Terry pleaded.

"But I have church business to attend to."

People around them on the platform were smirking and whispering. Terry looked at an elderly couple and exclaimed, "He's leavin' us with Uncle Cletus and Beezer."

"What?" said the old lady.

Sherry sniffled, "Our Pa's leavin' us with Uncle Cletus's talkin' Beezer."

"A talking beezer?" asked the shocked old lady.

Rev. Youngun tried to explain. "Beezer's a parrot, and—." The couple shook their heads and walked off. Terry climbed higher up Rev. Youngun's leg. "Calm down, Terry, I'll bring you something back."

Sherry let go of his arm, raised her arms in the air, and dashed around screaming, "No-o-o!"

Rev. Youngun was losing patience. "Sherry. Sherry, calm down. I'll bring you something too."

She stopped dead in her tracks and looked at her father. "Don't bring us back no monkeys!"

Uncle Cletus came up and stood beside them. Rev. Youngun

looked at his brother and said, "Cletus, I've got to be gettin' on this train. Take her, will you, please?" He handed Sherry over.

Uncle Cletus began stuttering, "Cer . . . cert . . . certain . . . okay!"

The eastbound train was preparing to leave and whistled loudly. "All aboard who's comin' aboard," the conductor shouted.

Rev. Youngun kissed each of the children, took his bag, and stepped toward the train door. "You all obey your uncle and be good children."

"Yes, Pa," they all said in unison.

As he stepped up into the train, he turned. "You've got nothin' to worry about. I'll be home before you know it." The train jumped forward, slowly pulling away. Rev. Youngun held on with one arm, waving good-bye, wondering how his life had gotten so complicated.

When the train was out of sight, Larry turned and stepped right into Annabell. "Excuse me," he stammered, flustered by her beautiful eyes.

"You don't need to make any excuses, handsome," she whispered.

"What'd you say?" Richie asked loudly. "Is this hayseed bothering you?" He glared, shoving Larry backward.

Father Walsh stepped between them. "What's goin' on here, boys?"

"Nothin', Father Walsh," Larry said. "Nothin' at all."

Father Walsh eyed them both, knowing that something had passed between them. "Well, let me introduce you. Larry Youngun, son of the Methodist minister of Mansfield, this is Richie Row, from the Monroe Street St. Louis Parish."

Larry hesitated, then stuck out his hand. Richie grudgingly

stuck out his, and they shook, each squeezing as hard as he could.

Father Walsh smiled. "You boys will be seeing a lot of each other. The Youngun children are going to be your guides when you go to Mr. Maurice Springer's farm tomorrow morning."

Richie sneered, "You can show us all 'bout milkin' the cows, farmboy."

Father Walsh pushed the Monroe Street Tigers along. "See you tomorrow, children. Okay, kids, everybody follow me. I don't want anyone getting lost."

Annabell winked at Larry. "See *you* tomorrow, valentine."

CHAPTER 19

CLETUS AND SHERRY

It took Cletus a long time to get the Younguns under control that first night. Terry and Sherry fought over everything and anything, mostly to keep from going to bed.

Finally, when it appeared he had everything under control, Cletus closed the boy's bedroom door quietly and crept toward the stairs.

"Uncle Cletus," Sherry called out softly.

"Yes?" he said, going to her door.

"Will you tell me a bedtime story?"

"It . . . it's kind of late."

"Please, just one story. That's what Pa always does."

Cletus went and sat on the end of her bed. She reached out her tiny hand and held his. "Tell me about when you were a little boy, you and Pa."

The darkness, the soft bed, and a request for a story took him back a lifetime. Back to when he was a little boy, off in a dark room, waiting for his father to come in and say prayers.

His father always went into Thomas's room first, where they said the prayers out loud together. Thomas who could recite pages from the Bible. Thomas who won the school poetry reading contest. Thomas who was the school's champion debater.

His father would stand in the hallway, looking into his brother's room. "You're a smart boy, Thomas Youngun, you're my pride and joy. When you speak, the whole world listens."

Cletus was back there in his mind. Crying in the dark, wishing his father would say that about him. *When I spoke, the whole world laughed,* he thought. *And they still do.*

Though it was never said directly, Cletus knew how disappointed his father was in him. It . . . it . . . it's not my fault," he would stutter, tears in his eyes.

"God works in mysterious ways," his father said, sitting on the edge of his bed. "Now let me say the prayers so you can go to sleep."

"Let me say the prayers," Father always said. It was never, "Cletus, let's say the prayers together." It was always "Let me say the prayers." Alone. So he wouldn't have to hear me stutter.

Sherry squeezed his hand. "Tell me a story."

"It . . . it . . . it's hard to tell a . . . a . . . a story with a . . . a . . . a . . ."

Sherry sat up and hugged him. "I love you just the way you are Uncle Cletus. I think you're nice."

"Tha . . . thanks," he whispered.

"How 'bout we say our prayers together. Like you did when you were a little boy."

Cletus looked at her soft smile in the moonlight. "I'd like th . . . th . . . that," he said.

Sherry took both his hands. "I'll take it real slow so you have time to get out the words, okay?"

Cletus nodded and Sherry began. "Now I lay me . . ." She stopped. "Uncle Cletus, let's say the prayer together."

Cletus squeezed her hands lightly. "Now I la . . . la . . .

lay me down to sleep . . ." The words just seemed to flow. *I wish my father was here,* he thought.

Sherry nodded against him as he finished the prayer. "You only stuttered once. I knew you could do it."

Long after Sherry was asleep, Cletus sat on the edge of the bed, trying to come to grips with the hurts from his past. Trying to understand and accept the way things were.

If I had children, he thought, *I'd accept them no matter how they were. I'd teach them to be kind and not laugh about things like stuttering. No one knows how hard it is to not be able to say clearly, "You hurt my feelings." Just a few words, so simple, yet so hard.*

CHAPTER 20

HOME TO THE PRAIRIE

Manly had gotten up well before dawn to get Laura's Oldsmobile ready for the trip. Pa wasn't happy about taking his final pioneer ride in a motor car, but he had no choice.

Manly had looked him square in the eye: "It's the car or nothin', Pa."

Pa grumbled. "This is the first time in my life when nothin' almost sounds better."

"It'll be fun, Pa," Laura said brightly over breakfast.

Pa shook his head. "'Bout as much fun as walkin' on nails."

Manly laughed. "At least this way you'll get where you're goin'—you can count on motor cars. Why, Laura's car has ten whole horsepower in it."

Pa closed his eyes. "Ain't no substitute for the real thing. Best horsepower in the world is four legs and a strong heart. Don't need gas or fixin' every five minutes."

Manly chuckled, shaking his head. "One day this whole country will be filled with motor cars. Everybody will be drivin' one."

Pa stood up and took his dishes to the sink. He turned to Manly and said quietly, "And everybody will be drivin' everybody crazy."

After breakfast Pa went out to inspect the motor car. Manly had filled it full of gas and put an extra can in the back. He'd put in a box of tools, food, clothes, and enough gadgets to start a whatnot shop. "You like bein' prepared, don't you, Manly?" Pa asked playfully.

"Be prepared and you can handle what comes. Yup, I do believe that," Manly answered, loading the last sack into the back.

Pa went in and got a few things he felt they might need on the road.

Laura had packed lightly, taking a small suitcase for the three or four days. Her long dress, lap robe, and dust veil made her look like anything but a pioneer.

Manly shook his head and chuckled. "You look like a movie pioneer at the nickelodeon, braving the hazards of a shopping spree."

Pa banged the porch door open. He looked as if he'd stepped out of the past in his homemade butternut brown pioneer pants, tall homemade boots, thick leather belt, and three-button, rough prairie workshirt.

On his side was a sheath knife. A rifle was slung on his back next to his bedroll and carrysack. With the pipe dangling from his mouth and the ear-to-ear grin on his face, you'd have thought he was a kid going on vacation.

"What you starin' at?" he said loudly to Laura and Manly.

"Why, Pa . . ." Laura stammered, "you look so . . ."

"How you want a pioneer to look?" Pa asked defensively.

"It's just . . ." Laura stammered again.

"You expect me to dress up like some fancy-dancy banker, goin' on a picnic? Land's sake, if you'd crossed the prairie thirty years ago dressed like that, you'd have never made it."

Manly saw the conversation was going nowhere. "Come on, you two, you best get goin' before the weather turns bad."

Pa looked toward the sky and sniffed the air. "I smell somethin' in the air."

Manly laughed. "It's probably all the food Laura packed."

"No, it smells like rain," Pa said, sniffing again.

Manly shook his head. "You best hope those storm clouds keep headin' east, or you two are goin' to get drenched."

"I brought umbrellas," Laura said, not realizing how silly she sounded.

Pa shook his head. "Never needed umbrellas in our wagons. We had covers on 'em, which is more than I can say 'bout this motor car." Taking the steps two at a time, Pa bounded up to the car and tossed his things into the back. Manly looked at the gun and knife.

"You plannin' on doin' a little huntin'?" Manly asked.

Pa grinned. "I'm goin' back to the prairie one last time, and I dreamed of doin' it the old way. Travelin' in a motor car like a couple of carpetbaggin' bankers lookin' for homesteads to mortgage and steal weren't never in my dreams."

"Times change, Pa," Manly laughed, winking at Laura.

"Yeah, well, you can keep the change, buddy—and here's your tip: just 'cause it's new don't make it good."

Laura started the engine, which popped and whizzed, then began purring. Manly patted the fender. "If the motor car had been invented fifty years ago, you'd have probably had twenty houses, the way you like to move around."

Pa chuckled. "No self-respectin' pioneer worth his weight in hardtack would have been caught ridin' in this contraption." He turned to Laura. "You ready?"

Laura said, "I'm as ready as I'm going to be." With a kiss to Manly, she started forward. "See you in a few days, Manly."

"Sure you got the map I made for you?" Manly shouted over the noise of the engine.

"Got it!" Laura laughed, pulling forward.

"You know where you're goin'?" he asked, walking alongside, a worried look on his face.

Laura looked at her pocket watch. "It's *only* eight. We should be past Springfield by noon."

Pa grabbed her pocket watch and tossed it to Manly. "You keep it! Where we're goin' I'm a-hopin' that time's stood still." Pa winked. "You got nothin' to worry 'bout, Manly. We're goin' *home. Home to the prairie!*" he shouted as Laura gunned the engine.

Manly watched them until they drove out of sight. He looked down at Jack the dog, who had come up and sat beside him. "Old fools and young fools . . . it don't get any worse than that."

As the car bumped along, Pa smiled. "Did you see what I stuck under the seat for you?" Laura tried to reach under, but swerved at the last moment to avoid hitting a mooing cow who'd wandered onto the road. Pa grabbed the door frame. "Be careful! We're goin' get killed 'fore we even get off your property."

"It's okay," Laura said, both hands on the wheel. "What'd you put under the seat?" Pa reached under and pulled out a sack. Inside was the dolly he'd brought her from De Smet. "Oh, Pa, I forgot to pack her."

"I didn't. And I brought you this," he said, pulling out one of her old, unused, nickel notepads and a stubby pencil.

"A diary pad? Why, I didn't even think to bring one."

"When you were my little pint of sweet cider half drunk up, you were always writin' 'bout everythin'."

Laura smiled, thinking about what he'd said, then gave him a playful frown. "Thought I was your little *half*-pint of sweet cider."

Pa laughed. "You're a grown-up woman. Think you're a full pint now."

Laura drove on for several minutes without saying anything, then turned. "And you forgot your fiddle."

"And you forgot your mind," Pa chuckled, pulling out the fiddle case from under the back seat. Opening it, he took out his fiddle and dug a note with the bow. "What you want to hear? 'Sweet Betsy From Pike'? 'Oh, My Darlin' Clementine'?"

He dipped the fiddle and began playing and singing,

Oh, Susanna, don't you cry for me,
For I went to Californie with a banjo on my knee.

Pa's fingers flew up and down the fiddle, and he winked and laughed as he sang. It was the perfect start for their journey back to find whatever they were both looking for.

Pa finished the song and stretched out his arm. "Look there," he said, pointing to the rolling Missouri countryside.

"It's beautiful, Pa."

"I've always said there's good land in the Missouras for a poor man to build a home. Heck, there's 'nough room in Missoura, Kansas, and Arkansas to house all the good folks in this country."

Laura laughed and took off her scarf, letting her hair fly in the wind. They weren't in a wagon, but the traveling feeling was there. The wind, the wide-open spaces, and the general feeling of being free invigorated them both.

Along the way they laughed, joked, and talked of old times. From Mansfield they journeyed through Seymour, Rogersville, and places too small to have a name. Laura's goal was to make it to Joplin, Missouri, by nightfall, if all went well.

On the east side of Springfield, two Buicks with cow-horn hood ornaments and advertising banners on the side came speeding past them, tooting their horns.

"Did you read those banners?" Laura smiled.

Pa fumbled for his glasses. "What they say?"

"Read it yourself."

Pa peered ahead but frowned. "Can't. They're too far away. Speed up a bit, will ya'?"

Laura pressed the accelerator and caught up with the two Buicks.

WILL ROGERS
will arrive at the Springfield Theatre,
FRIDAY, February 13th, and do his show,
"Two Wagons—Both Covered"
With "Ponjolla" singing.
America's funniest pioneer.

As she passed the first one, Pa squinched his eyes, read the sign, then smiled. "I like that Will Rogers, don't you?"

"He's a funny man."

Pa peered ahead, but couldn't make out the second one. "Hurry up! Let's see what the next one says. Maybe it's got one of his jokes on it or somethin'."

As Laura accelerated, Pa sat back, smiling. "Yes, sir, that Will Rogers makes me want to split a gut. Did you hear the one he said about . . ." Pa paused as the second sign came into view.

IN 1869 PIONEERS RODE IN OLD COVERED WAGONS
NOW
EVERY TRUE PIONEER RIDES IN A BUICK
AREN'T YOU GLAD YOU DRIVE A BUICK?

Pa slowly shook his head. "It's a shame that the glory days of America are now reduced to some advertisin' slogan or those tall tales in the nickel movies."

"Everyone knows the movies are make-believe," Laura laughed.

"You be surprised how many people think moving pictures are gospel. The real West was the one we saw lookin' out through wax-papered windows." He played a note, then stopped. "What was the first Western movie you ever saw?"

Laura thought for a moment. "I think it was *The Great Train Robbery.*"

Pa put the fiddle down and reached into his leather case. He pulled out another aging, folded broadside. He opened it up and showed her the title, *The Cowboy Kid.*

She shrugged. "I didn't see that one. Who starred in it? William Hart? Bronco Billy?"

"Naw, some kid who had the whole audience jumpin' up and down in their seats, watchin' the squirt carry 'round a six-gun bigger 'n' he was." Pa put the broadside back and asked, "Want to hear a song I wrote after I saw it?"

"Sure." She smiled.

"It's called, 'City Cowboys,' and . . ." He dug out the first notes with his bow. "It goes like this. A-one, a-two, a-one two three, well. . . ." Pa's voice held the first note, then he began:

> Well, bein' a city cowboy just ain't no fun
> When there ain't no horses around.
> And ridin' the range is kind of rough
> When asphalt is your huntin' ground.
> Well, I read all the books and seen the shows,
> But I ain't never seen a tumbleweed.

Lord just once I'd like to look in the mirror
And see a cowboy smilin' back at me.

'Cause I'm an old cowhand,
Who ain't never seen the Rio Grande.
I'm an old cowhand,
Who ain't never seen the Rio Grande.

Pa stopped and laughed. "That's just the first verse. I wrote a whole song 'bout all the kids and old folks ridin' their movie seats up and down like they was cowboys."

"You ought to record that song, Pa. Have Sears sell it."

Pa shrugged. "There are a lot of things I ought to do or should have done."

CHAPTER 21

WELCOME TO THE COUNTRY

The Younguns awoke early because it was the day to show the new kids from St. Louis around. Larry and Terry had schemed all night. "That red-haired kid shouldn't have called us hicks and hayseeds!" Larry said, making a fist.

"What's a hick?" Sherry asked. "You mean a hiccup?"

"No, no." Larry frowned. "A hick's a hayseed."

"What's a hayseed?" Terry asked, wanting to know why he should be mad.

Larry slapped his forehead. "A person like us, who's raised in the country."

"What's wrong with that?" Terry asked, scratching his head.

"Nothin' when we say it," Larry exclaimed. "But he's sayin' we're dumbos."

Terry jumped around the room, fighting his shadow with air punches. "Let me at 'em— Let me at 'em—"

Uncle Cletus looked into their room. "Ready for br . . . brea . . . food?"

"No," Larry said, speaking for all of them, "we're gonna skip breakfast this morning."

Cletus was disappointed. "But I ma . . . cooked some har . . . round chicken things."

"Use 'em for paperweights," Terry whispered.

"Wh . . . what? I didn't hear you," Cletus said.

Larry put his hand over Terry's mouth. "He said we'll take a bag of 'em to the barn and eat 'em while we do our chores."

"Great!" Cletus said, very happy that they were going to eat the breakfast he'd worked so hard on. He went back to the kitchen to put some eggs in a sack.

"Why'd you tell him that?" Terry said. "We can't even feed those death balls to Crab Apple. Might kill him."

"We'll just drop 'em down the outhouse on the way to the barn."

Larry and Terry used the time before the 10:00 A.M. arrival of the St. Louis kids to prepare a special welcome. Terry fed Crab Apple nothing but cucumbers, and Sherry gathered up a small bucket of rabbit droppings, chicken and bird feathers, and some of the hard road apples that their mule and horse had dropped in the field.

Patting her on the head, Larry said, "Now put the rabbit droppings on a plate, sprinkle powdered sugar on 'em, and cover 'em with a napkin. Pick out the best road apples and put 'em in a bowl with a little honey on 'em. And put that big meadow muffin on a platter."

He turned to Terry. "You take a few of them road apples and stick twigs and feathers in 'em."

"What for?" Terry asked.

Larry laughed. "So we can show them how Missouri hayseeds treat city slickers. We'll give 'em some prehistoric Missouri birds for gifts."

"Where you goin'?" Terry shouted out as Larry pulled down the tall ladder.

"None of your bees-ness," he laughed.

Larry put the ladder against the back wall and carefully lifted the thirty-inch hornet's nest from the roof corner of the barn. The hornets were still sluggish from the cold weather, so it was relatively easy for Larry to lacquer it up. When he finished, some of the hornets were awake inside, buzzing around trying to get out.

Sherry and Terry cut hair off the tail of Larry's horse, Lightning, and tied it onto Dangit the dog's back. Larry painted white stripes on Crab Apple with some old fence paint, and though it took a while, they were finally able to strap a small set of goat horns onto Teddy Roosevelt the turkey's head.

"You guys ready to go?" Larry shouted out.

"You bet!" Terry shouted.

Larry grinned and nodded, looking at the menagerie of animals looking like something from a storybook.

Sherry wiggled her nose back and forth. "Why'd we paint stripes on ol' Crab Apple? Mules don't got stripes."

Larry took a deep breath. "I told you, when we get to Mr. Springer's farm, Crab Apple's a zebra and . . ." he looked at Dangit, shaking the horse hair on his back. ". . . and Dangit's a hummin' goat, and . . ."

Terry looked at Teddy Roosevelt the turkey, trying to shake the goat horns loose. "What's Teddy Roosevelt again?"

Larry spit. "Dummy, I told you he's a Deer-key, a rare Missouri half-deer, half-turkey." He looked at Sherry. "You got the raisins and dried apples ready?"

"Yup," she laughed, pulling back the cover over the plates, showing how she'd arranged the rabbit and horse droppings.

"Got them prehistoric Missouri birds?" he asked Terry.

"You bet!" Terry laughed, opening up a box of horse droppings with sticks and feathers stuck into them to look like birds.

Larry laughed. "Let's go give them city boys a real welcome to the country—hayseed style!"

So they headed to Maurice's farm, each animal pulling a miniature homemade cart behind it. The Younguns were hicks bearing gifts, looking for fun.

Terry peeked into the box with the buzzing sound and closed the cover. "What you call this lacquered-up hornet's nest again?"

Larry winked. "That's a rare giant Mexican jumpin' bean. We're gonna let 'em take it home as a gift."

"They better 'bee' careful," Terry laughed.

The Monroe Street Tigers sat on the back of the hay wagon, looking around Mansfield's Main Street. Chew-Chew sat between Richie's legs.

Richie pushed his latest-fashion driving cap back and shook his head. "Guess this is what they mean by a one-horse town."

Burpo stared at the smiling people on the streets. "Ain't nothin' to do around here except eat sardines." At his loud burp everyone on the wagon groaned and held his nose.

"I hope they got a lot of food to eat," Rollo grunted, "cause *I'm* still hungry."

Annabell laughed. "Hungry? You ate and drank everythin' in the parish hall."

Father Walsh, sitting up front beside Maurice, turned around. "Children, you must sit down. We're going five miles an hour, and you might fall off and get hurt!" He turned to Maurice. "Thanks for picking us up in your wagon. These kids have never had the pleasure of a hayride."

"Wait 'til they get to the farm," Maurice chuckled, not knowing what the Younguns had in store. "Rev. Youngun's kids told me they wanted to show these St. Louie kids 'round the farm all by themselves."

Father Walsh smiled, nodding. "You know, you can always count on the Methodists to be civil to Catholics. Don't you agree, Maurice?"

Maurice nodded. "These Youngun kids are good children. Real kind, just like their daddy. You can *count* on that."

"Good," Father Walsh smiled. "I want these children to have a real country experience."

The Younguns had hidden all their gifts and special animals behind Maurice's barn and were standing at the driveway waving as if they were welcoming home old friends.

Richie snickered. "Look at them hayseeds. I told you we'd be leadin' 'em around by the nose."

"Yeah, call them names and they come back for more," Burpo chuckled.

Annabell looked at her fellow Tigers and then at the Younguns. She felt a little uneasy.

Maurice stopped the wagon, and Father Walsh's smile stretched from Mansfield back to Ireland. "Aye, little Younguns, thank you for being good enough to show your city cousins what farm life is like."

Larry nodded solicitously and put on a real hick tone of voice. "We all just glad that they comin' to see how we country folk lives. Ain't we?" he asked, turning to his brother and sister.

"We sure is!" they both responded simultaneously.

Maurice eyeballed them, trying to figure out what they were up to. "You Younguns ready to show these kids 'round my farm?"

Larry did his best aw-shucks, slapping his hat on his leg. "Ready? Why, we've been ready for hours!"

"That's good, 'cause I want to take Father Walsh for a horse-back ride up over Devil's Ridge."

"Where?" Father Walsh asked, quite taken aback.

"Oh, Father," Maurice laughed, "that's just what it's called. Shaped like a devil's horn, that's all."

Larry smiled. "You two go on ridin' and we'll teach 'em *all-ll* 'bout farm life."

Richie leaned over and whispered to the rest of the Tigers, "I bet these hicks even got gifts for us." As the St. Louis children got off, Richie sneered at Larry, "I want *you* to show *me* around, okay?" Chew-Chew sat beside him, growling at Larry.

Larry smiled. *"You're* just the one *I* wanted to show 'round. No hard feelins for yesterday, okay?"

"Yeah, you're all right, I guess," Richie said. "You didn't rat on me when you had the chance." He slapped Larry on the back as hard as he could. "Come on, country boy, show me how you live!"

Something came over Larry when he looked up into Annabell's eyes. She smiled back. As Larry reached out his hand and helped her from the wagon, her long hair and hint of perfume wafted across his face.

Richie's mouth was hanging open. "Keep your hands off her!" he said, stepping forward.

Larry smiled. "Just helpin' the lady down, that's all—Cuz."

Richie watched Larry walk away and turned to Annabell. "Watch out for him," he warned.

"I got to watch nothin'!" Annabell replied crossly. You and me are just friends. I don't got to do what you tell me to do! That's what my mother did, and all she ever got for thanks was a hard slap from my dad!"

She walked off in a huff, leaving Richie in her dust. Larry had seen it all and shook his head. He whispered to himself, "Boy-oh-boy! She's just like a wild mustang."

The Younguns played for time while Maurice and Father Walsh saddled up. Maurice still couldn't figure them out and leaned over to Larry. "Be *nice* to these kids. Don't go doin' nothin' silly, okay?"

"We'll be nice." He slapped the rump of Maurice's horse. "Now go on and ride. We've got to show these kids around."

When they had ridden out of sight, Larry and Terry pushed hay bales in a half-circle around an old wagon bed next to the barn. He whispered to Terry, "You and Sherry start bringing out the animals as I call 'em out."

His brother and sister scampered back around the barn. Larry stepped up onto the wagon bed and whistled for attention. "Come sit on the hay bales! We're gonna sing a country song."

"Oh, man," Richie grumbled, "we came all the way from St. Louis for this?"

"Shhhh!" said Annabell. "This might be fun."

"Everyone know 'Old MacDonald Had a Farm'?"

The other parish kids screamed, "Yes!" but the Tigers just nodded.

"Great!" Larry nodded. "As we sing it, all call out the animals, and my brother will bring 'em out to show you. Okay?"

The parish kids were very excited—only Rollo looked upset. He raised his hand. "Got anythin' to eat? I'm starvin'!"

Larry nodded sympathetically. "Sure, we got some special treats for you to take back to the parish with you." He turned and waved his arm. "Sherry, Terry, show 'em the *homemade* country treats!"

Rollo licked his lips as the sugar-covered rabbit droppings were put in front of him. "What are they?" he asked Sherry.

"Missouri raisins," she answered with a big, bright smile. "But you can't eat 'em now."

Burpo picked up a honey-coated horse dropping. "What's this? Never seen anythin' like it. Got any with sardines?"

Terry smiled. "Well, that's what we call a Missouri Road Apple—and it'll probably taste real good with sardines."

"What's on the big platter?" Burpo asked.

"That's a fresh meadow muffin. We've prepared it special for you to take back to St. Louis with you," Larry said, looking down at the candy sticks from Terry's special stash that were sticking out from the top. Larry whistled, "Okay, kids, let's sing. Ready?"

Annabell winked at Larry, and he blushed so hard he lost his voice for a moment. "Ah . . . ah . . . ah." he stammered.

"What's wrong with that big blond-headed kid?" Richie asked Annabell.

She shrugged. "I don't know. Maybe a cat got his tongue."

Larry regained his composure, "Here we go . . .

> Old MacDonald had a farm, ey-yi-ey-yi-o.
> And on that farm he had a . . .

Larry nodded to Terry.

> . . . a humming goat,
> E-yi-e-yi-o.

Terry came walking out with Dangit, who was none too pleased, shaking the horse hair back and forth. Sherry walked behind him, pointing to Dangit and telling everyone, "He's from Korea."

Larry was waving his arms for the kids to sing along, but most were just staring dumbly at the humming goat.

> With a hum-hum here,
> And a hum-hum there . . .

After the first verse, he kept the song going,

> *And on that farm he had a **Deer-key**,*

Larry winked and nodded to Sherry, who brought out Teddy Roosevelt, the turkey, with the goat horns on his head.

> E-yi-e-yi-o.
> With a deer-dear here,
> And a key-key there . . .

Terry Roosevelt strutted his stuff behind Sherry while Larry kept singing as loud as he could. Larry nodded to Terry, who reached behind the barn for Crab Apple's reins and pulled the reluctant mule forward.

> *And on that farm he had a*
> ***Zebra,***
> *E-yi-e-yi-o.*

The parish kids were all wide-eyed at the sight of the *zebra* in front of them. Burpo leaned over and whispered to Richie, "Zebra? Thought zebras lived in Africa."

Richie shrugged. "Maybe the guy who owns the farm is an African."

Terry paraded Crab Apple the zebra around, feeding him a big cucumber. One of the kids touched him and got white paint on his fingers. Terry just shook his head and said, "Be careful—this is molting season for zebras."

Up on the wagon bed, Larry continued with the song.

> With a zee-zee here
> And a zee-zee there,
> Here a zee . . .

When Terry got in front of Richie, he stopped and smiled. "This is a Missouri zebra."

"Oh, yeah?" Richie asked, pulling his driving cap forward, eyeballing the "zebra."

"Feel his tail." Terry smiled.

The moment Richie touched his tail, Crab Apple kicked him backward over the hay bale. All the parish kids were rolling on the ground in laughter. Even Annabell was snickering.

Richie dusted off his hat. "Get that zebra out of my face, shrimp!"

"Yeah," sneered Burpo, "beat it before I murderize you!"

Terry dropped Crab Apple's reins and dove headfirst into Burpo's stomach. No one was listening to Larry sing. They were all gathered around the two sparring little boys. Behind them Chew-Chew started growling at Dangit the humming goat.

Larry jumped down to break it up, but Richie stepped into his path. "Let 'em fight," he snarled.

Larry grabbed Richie's arm and pushed him aside. "No fightin' 'round here, Cuz."

Larry jumped back on the hay bale, holding Terry with one arm. "Fightin's not good. We're all friends! As a matter of fact, we've got a gift for each of you."

The parish kids shivered with anticipation. "What'd you get us?" a small boy asked.

Terry struggled free from Larry and straightened out his shirt. He smiled at the Irish boy, "We got you each a prehistoric fossil."

"A what?" asked Rollo. "Can you eat it?"

"Naw," Larry laughed, holding up one of the "fossil" road apples. "This is a piece of history, dropped down on the ground and preserved. We want each of you to take one home with you to remember your country friends by."

Terry and Sherry pulled out the cart with the horse apples. "What kind of fossil is it?" Richie asked, looking at the feathers sticking out.

Sherry smiled. "These are prehistoric Missouri birds—just for you!"

Larry saw Maurice and Father Walsh riding up, so he whistled for attention. "Kids, kids! Put them away. We didn't make enough for Father Walsh."

Terry whispered to Larry, "What 'bout the . . . ?" he said, pointing to the box with the lacquered-up hornet's nest.

"Oh yeah." Larry nodded to his brother. He raised up his hands. "And kids, we've got a special gift for Red and his friends," Larry said, pointing to Richie and the Tigers. "To show you that there's no hard feelings."

"What is it? Can you eat it?" Rollo asked.

"Naw," Larry said, shaking his head. "It's a rare giant Mexican jumpin' bean."

He opened up the box and held it up. Several of the hornets were buzzing around inside, trying to get out.

"Sounds like it's ready to jump," said Burpo.

"Oh, you'll know when to jump—er, I mean you'll know when it's going to jump," Larry smiled. He saw that Maurice and Father Walsh were almost to the end of the drive. "Hurry now, put away your gifts."

The parish kids circled around Father Walsh, who began describing his horse ride. Maurice rode up in front of Larry, Terry, and Sherry.

Maurice looked at Crab Apple with his white stripes. He looked at Teddy Roosevelt with the horns on his head. And he looked at Dangit with the horse hair tied onto his back. *They've been up to something!* he thought.

Larry looked down and started to speak, but Maurice held up his hand. "I don't even want to hear about it. No, sir, don't want to hear nothin' you little Methodists got to say. Uh-uh, no way. Just don't do nothin' more 'til they leave."

Maurice took a quick look at Father Walsh, then looked Larry in the eye. "Has Father Walsh seen these whatever-they-ares?" Larry shook his head. Maurice grunted, "Good! Now get them behind the barn and hope that he don't." He added, "You kids should be ashamed of yourselves, treatin' guests this way. Your Pa ought to whip the tar outta you. Yes, sir, might just do it myself."

The parish kids were piled onto the back of the hay wagon, singing the new words to "Old MacDonald." Chew-Chew looked over the edge of the wagon, growling at Dangit, who was looking out from behind the barn.

Father Walsh walked over and handed the reins of the horse to Maurice. "Maurice, the kids said they had a great time."

He stopped as the kids sang out, ". . . And on his farm he had a zebra."

Father Walsh shook his head. "Some of them think you have a zebra on this farm. Don't kids have great imaginations?"

Maurice just nodded, rolling his eyes when the priest turned to leave.

CHAPTER 22

HONKY TONKIN'

Laura and Pa were acting like kids, looking and laughing at everything. It was like old times again until they approached Sarcoxie, Missouri. The engine began smoking, so Laura and Pa looked for a creek.

Laura pulled off the road when Pa spotted a little brook next to a ramshackle old house. Pa filled up the radiator, and they were on their way. Down the road were Indian mounds, and Pa rode past in silence, bowing his head slightly. Pointing to the mounds, he said, "That's 'bout all that's left of Indians 'round here."

"What's that, Pa?"

"Bones. Just bones. You know, we drove all the Indians out of the Ozarks. They'd been here since before the year 940, 'cording to a book I read. They were here to greet De Soto himself 'round 1541."

"What was the tribe's name?" Laura asked.

"The Missouris, girl. Don't you know your history? The Missouris were the mother tribe for the Iowa, Kansas, Osage, Quawpaw, Arkansas, and other tribes everythin' round here's named after."

"What happened to them all?"

"Things went fine until the white man started movin' into here 'round 1803. Seems the Indians thought we were a bad influence on the young redskins, so in 1810, they went to William Clark, who—"

Laura interrupted him. "You mean *the* William Clark of the Lewis and Clark expedition?"

"If you'd just quit interruptin' me, I'd have told you that it was the same Clark. He became governor of the territory. The Indians offered to leave their beautiful Missouri lands and move out into the great desert if the white chiefs in Washington would agree never to distrub them or invade their desert lands."

Laura thought for a moment, then looked at Pa. "Desert? Where was the great desert they moved to?"

Pa looked at the passing countryside. "Where we're goin' to. They called the prairie the great desert."

"Why'd you move us there?"

Pa shrugged. "My cousin, Senator Ingalls, said that it was okay, that the Indians would just give up and move out like they'd done all the other times."

"But they didn't."

"And we were forced to move. Either the Indians were goin' to burn us out, or the government was goin' to evict us."

He looked down and rubbed his eyes. "Our days there started so good and ended so bad. Drums beatin' all night, till you felt you were goin' crazy. The soldiers demanding that we leave or they'd knock our house down."

Laura gripped the wheel. "I can remember those nights of drums, Pa. You sat up until dawn with your rifle in your lap. It was scary."

In his mind's eye, Pa saw it again as he spoke to Laura. "Settlers like us broke the agreement the Indians had with the government. They'd given up their ancestral homes and huntin' grounds in the Missouris for the great desert. Then we came along and built our house smack dab on the edge of their land. If I'd just stopped three miles east, we'd have been all right. But there was always somethin' greener down the road for me."

"Were you scared, Pa?" Laura asked in a quiet voice.

Pa nodded. "We'd been havin' our fences pulled down and livestock stolen. It was happenin' to all the neighbors. Indians were tellin' us to get out while the gettin' was good." He sighed, "Most of us thought we could tough it out. But then the killin' started."

Laura closed her eyes and shivered at the thought.

"Then one night Indians banded up 'round the house. I was asleep on my feet. Hadn't slept in 'bout five nights with the drums and all."

As he spoke, Laura began to remember that night. She could see herself, huddled in the corner. Covering her ears, trying to stop the sound of the drums.

"So I just strapped on my bullet belt and told Ma, 'I'm gonna fight 'em 'til I'm dead.' " Pa paused, rubbing his eyes. "Your ma tried to stop me, but like a fool I barged right over and opened the door. Facing me was 'bout ten of the meanest lookin' men I'd ever seen, all painted up."

Pa looked at Laura. "And my little half pint of sweet cider, you came up behind me and . . ."

Laura remembered it all, "I . . . I screamed. I screamed because I thought they were goin' to kill us."

"That *was* their plan."

"And they had scalps." Laura said, shaking her head, "I remember the long blond-haired woman's scalp."

Pa interrupted her. "And red and brown and black . . . it

was a horrible sight. Ten–twenty scalps hangin' from their belts, some still drippin' blood. They were bloodthirsty savages comin' to take our scalps."

"Why didn't they kill us?" Laura shivered.

Pa shrugged. "Your Ma saved us. I was ready to fight defendin' my family, but Ma was the smart one."

"What'd she do, Pa?"

"Your ma just grabbed up her fresh baked bread and got between me and the Indians. They looked at her like she was crazy, but she began breaking off pieces, eatin' some and puttin' 'em into the Indian's hands. I think they were so shocked that they just left us alone."

"I remember they smelled awful," Laura said, shivering at the memory.

"You'd smell too if you were wearin' fresh skunk skins for pants," Pa laughed.

Laura and Pa rode in silence, each thinking their own thoughts about those last days in the prairie house, when the drums of death turned their world upside down.

Laura again thought of those Indians, standing in their house. She remembered their leather moccasins, their red-brown legs, and the knives and tomahawks hanging from the thongs that held up the skunk skins.

Their faces at the time seemed fierce, their features strange. She had never been close to an Indian and marveled at how their black eyes glittered. With their heads shaved except for a long pony tail standing almost straight up from the center of their heads, laced with feathers, it was a sight she would never forget.

It wasn't only Ma's bread they took. They also ate all the cornbread, meat and stole Pa's tobacco and other odds and ends they fancied. Pa stood and watched them take what they wanted.

Now Laura looked at her father. "Would they have killed us, Pa?"

"What? Who?" Pa asked, a bit startled from his own thoughts.

"The Indians who came into our house. Would they have killed us?"

"Maybe. There were a lot of settlers dyin' over silly things like tobacco. When I saw that they took kindly to your Ma givin' 'em that bread, I knew that we were better off lettin' 'em take a few things than have 'em leave with our scalps. It was better not to make enemies of 'em, which is maybe why we got out alive."

"I'm glad they didn't come back."

"So am I," Pa laughed, "I'd have lost my appitite tryin' to eat with a bunch of fresh killed skunk skins in the room. Whew! That was 'bout the worst thing I'd ever smelled."

Outside of Joplin, they had their first flat. Pa got down and looked at the tire. "Still don't know why they didn't put wooden wheels on these motor cars 'stead of these flimsy rubber things."

Laura ignored him. "It won't take more than an hour to fix it, if we both work at it." But an hour became two before the solid tubed tire finally slipped on. Pa sat on the car step, head hung down.

"You going to be okay, Pa?" Laura asked, concerned about his heart.

"Just a bit dizzy. Let me rest here a minute, will ya?"

"How about we have some lunch? Maybe you need to eat something." Laura's voice died off as the pill bottle appeared in Pa's hand.

He took one of his pills, sipping water from his old canteen. "I'll feel better in a few minutes. Shouldn't have done all that work on the tire. Wore myself out."

He breathed deeply, resting against the car. "You know," he wheezed, "it's a funny thing 'bout age. Kids just can't wait to get older, and old folks just want to get younger."

"Just human nature." Laura nodded.

"I'll tell you one thing. Everyone thinks like Ponce de Leon when they start headin' toward heaven's gate."

"Wouldn't a fountain of youth be nice?" Laura smiled, aware that Pa was talking about his own worries.

Pa nodded. "Worst thing 'bout gettin' older is fear. When you're young, you don't fear nothin', not a thing. But when you get old, you fear goin' to sleep 'cause you might not wake up. You fear losing your friends and family. You fear goin' to funerals and walkin' past graveyards. You fear runnin' out of money, livin' alone, or havin' the sum total of your life add up to failure."

Laura looked up to the darkening sky and buttoned her collar. "We best get going, Pa. We've still got a ways to go before we get to Joplin."

Thunder cracked overhead, and the first raindrops began to fall. "This thing got a top?" Pa asked, looking up toward the clouds.

Laura started the engine, and the car pulled forward with a jump. "No, just a parking cover to keep dust out."

"Well," Pa said, buttoning up his jacket, "don't have to worry 'bout no dust gettin' in here." The rain fell harder, and he pulled his hat down. "No, sir, no dust in this pioneer's car—maybe a flood, but no dust."

Laura pointed to the back floorboard. "There are some umbrellas back there."

Pa reached back, grumbling, "Umbrellas, rubber tires—this ain't no pioneer's ride. This is a circus trip."

Opening the umbrella, he held it over Laura's head, but with the wind and the pouring rain, it didn't do much good. They were soon soaked.

A big gust of wind pulled the umbrella from his hand, and it flew into the trees. "Got any other bright ideas?" Pa grinned, his face dripping with rain. Before she could answer, a crude, hand-painted sign appeared:

PRAIRIE SALOON AND DANSE HALL
GOOD BOOZE, BAND, AND EATS

"Let's pull in there," Pa shouted over the wind.

"Into a honky-tonk?" Laura asked with shock. "It can't be much further." Another crude sign came into view.

PRAIRIE SALOON
LAST STOP FOR TWENTY MILES
EAT NOW OR DONT GRIPE!

Pa shrugged. "I'm cold, hungry, and gettin' in a bad mood in this uncovered motorized wagon. I vote we pull in and wait out the rain."

Laura answered, "But, Pa! It's a saloon!"

"Laurie, Laurie. The first place built in every prairie town— the first *ten* places built in every prairie town—were saloons. After that, if there was any more wood left, they built a church or school." He shook his head. "I've had you in a saloon before."

"You have?"

"We stopped at 'em along the prairie to get supplies and

such. We lived right next to one in the Dakotas. Trust me—we'll just wait out the rain and get ourselves some food—like a big, thick steak."

Laura shook her head. "I vote we don't go."

Pa shrugged. "Vote's two to one for pullin' in."

"Two to one? There's only two of us that I see in this car," she said, shaking off the rain in her hair.

Pa grinned: "There's you, there's me, and then there's the me who's your pa. Me and Pa voted to pull over. That's two to one, so . . ." he paused, smiling in the rain, ". . . you lose."

Around the bend the lights from the windows of the wayside saloon lit up the dark road. Laura pulled into the muddy, half-flooded parking area. She squeezed the car under the eaves of the building, and she and Pa managed to pull the cover over the seats.

Pa helped her up onto the porch and looked through the windows. Things were going full-swing inside, with farmers clogging and jigging around the sawdust dance floor to the tune of a four-piece country band.

As he opened the door, he whispered to Laura, "Just act natural, and no one'll know that you're a stick-in-the-mud young biddy."

"Pa!" she exclaimed. "I am not!"

Pa looked at the happy crowd and shook his head. "Don't become an old crow 'fore your time. Take away the booze, and this is like all the jiggin' parties your grandma used to throw back in Wisconsin."

A farmer in his Sunday best winked at Laura. "But Pa, I'm a married woman."

"There's nothin' wrong with people havin' fun, Laurie. You and Manly been workin' so hard for so long that you've forgotten how we danced and sang across the prairie. You've forgotten how to have fun."

They found a table on the edge of the dance floor, and Pa ordered thick rare steaks, baked potatoes, and milk. The painted-up waitress nodded at the order until he said "milk."

"Did you say milk?" she asked, as if he'd said a foreign word.

Pa laughed. "Yeah, I'll take it straight up in a jigger and my—" he looked at Laura and winked. "My girl will have her milk on the rocks, if you got any, or in a nice cold beer mug."

It was hard to talk with the noise from the band, so they ate in silence, listening to the band and watching the dancers. Then, with an offbeat drum roll, the singer held up his hands.

"Folks, you know tonight is amateur night. We call it singin' for your supper, 'cause the winner gets his dinner free."

Pa raised his eyebrows, then looked at the bill the waitress had just brought him. She stood behind him, hovering like a vulture.

"Could you come back in a minute?" Pa asked.

"Somethin' wrong?" the waitress grumbled.

"I left somethin' in the car," Pa said, standing up to leave.

The waitress eyeballed him. "We arrest deadbeats 'round here." Laura nervously fidgeted with her hands.

Pa took a deep breath. "I ain't gonna skip out. I just forgot somethin' in the car, so why don't you trot back over to the bar and bring us back double milks, okay?" Laura giggled as the waitress walked away mumbling.

The rain had let up to a soft drizzle, so Pa walked along under the porch eave, reached under the car cover, and brought out his fiddle. As he walked back into the saloon, the singer was shouting out, "Okay, here's our first singin' contestant," He pointed to a scraggly blonde wearing a homemade dress and muddy boots. "She calls herself Pretty Girl Carter, and she's gonna sing 'Sweet Betsy From Pike.' "

The crowd whistled, and Pretty Girl Carter opened her mouth to smile. She was missing her two front teeth. The crowd hooted and catcalled at her terrible-looking smile.

Pa sat back down as Pretty Girl began to sing. He whispered to Laura, "She don't need a spoon to eat—she needs a broom!"

"Broom?"

"Yeah," Pa laughed, "with that gaping hole in her mouth, she could just bite down on the edge of the table and you could sweep the food into her mouth."

"Oh, Pa. She's just missing a few teeth."

Pretty Girl missed her high notes, and Pa winced. "She looks a jack-o'-lantern and sings like a crow."

Laura looked under the table and saw Pa's violin case. "Why'd you go get your fiddle?"

"Just wanted to . . . got it for the depends."

"Depends?" she asked over the grating high notes of the off-key toothless singer.

Pa shrugged. "Yeah. Depends on whether I want to pay this dinner bill or get up there and win this contest."

The crowd clapped politely for Pretty Girl and the next three contestants. One sang, one danced, and one demonstrated how to call the pigs while singing, "She'll Be Comin' 'Round the Mountain."

The waitress came up. "You ready to pay, Old-Timer?"

Pa looked down and thought, *Old-Timer?* The singer held up his hands for silence. "Is there anyone else who wants to sing for his supper?"

Pa winked at Laura. "Well, here goes nothin'." He stepped onto the dance floor.

"What about my money?" the waitress asked loudly.

"I'm gonna try singin' for the bill. If that don't work, I'll flip you for it—maybe even double or nothin'!"

The singer saw Pa walking toward him. "And it looks like we have one more contestant." He reached out his hand and pulled Pa onto the makeshift stage. "What's your name, Old-Timer?"

Pa made a face and looked around. "Must be someone 'round here that looks like me, cause you're the second person in two minutes that's called me Old-Timer."

A few in the audience got the joke, and the singer smiled. "Well, traveler, what's your name?"

Pa saw Laura watching. She winked at him and suppressed a laugh behind her hand. Pa smiled. "My name's Fiddlin' Pa, and I got a song to earn my supper."

"What's the song?" asked the singer.

Pa turned and smiled at the band. "You boys will know this one." Pa dug his bow deep into the opening rift of the song and shouted out to the crowd, "It's called 'The Arkansas Traveler!' " The crowd began to cheer and clap in time to the music.

An old man got up and did a pigeon wing, and a couple of single women got up and jigged. Laura clapped along as Pa played and sang like a man on fire.

A man asked Laura to dance, but she shook her head no, content to move her feet up and down under the table. She loved watching Pa's blue eyes sparkling under the light while his bow danced over the strings.

Every time he finished a song, the crowd cheered for more. He played "Irish Washerwoman," "Devil's Hornpipe," and the "Money Musk." Everyone was dancing, even the lights that twinkled around the room.

Pa noticed another man asking Laura to dance, so he jigged

over to her table. "Get up and dance with me before some man grabs you!"

Laura tried to protest, but Pa worked her backward on the dance floor like a sheepdog moving his herd and forced her to jig with him while he played the chorus from the song. Laura's feet moved faster and faster, heels going clickety-clack, clickety-clack.

Soon there was a circle around Laura and Pa, clapping faster and faster to match her feet. Sweat was running down Pa's face as fast as his fingers were dancing up and down the fiddle's neck.

When Pa finished, the crowd cheered for more, so he raised his hands. "Here's one for the old days," he said, swinging around to the band. "Play 'Dixie,' boys. Tonight, the South's gonna rise again!"

The whole room was on its feet, singing and dancing, screaming rebel yells, as Pa and his wondrous fiddle sang a fast-paced version of the southern anthem:

> In Dixieland where I was born,
> Early, Lord, one frosty morn,
> Look away, look away, look away, Dixieland.

The crowd wanted more, and by the second rendition, the singer declared Pa the winner. "You earned your supper, Fiddlin' Pa!" he laughed. "You're the fiddlin'est fool who's ever played here!"

Pa thanked the crowd and smiled as people patted him on the back when he walked to his table. Laura laughed and hugged him. "Oh, Pa, you were great!"

Pa laughed. "And you can still move those feet. You ain't such a stick-in-the-mud after all."

The waitress walked up to the table. "What you want me to do with this two-dollar bill for your dinner and milk?"

Pa smiled. "The man said dinner for us is on the house, so give the bill to him."

Pa finished off Laura's glass of milk and wiped his moustache. "Come on," he said, grabbing her arm, "let's get on outta here."

"But what about a tip? I got to pay your bill," the waitress asked.

"You do?" Laura asked.

"Yeah," the waitress said, shaking her head. "House rules. If the winner's at your table, you got to cover the dinner."

Laura softened. "You have any children?"

"Two little ones. My old man run off with another waitress 'bout six months ago. Ain't heard from him since."

Pa looked at the waitress under the harsh lights and saw the hard times she'd been through. He'd stopped in the honky-tonk, had a good meal, had an even better time playing his fiddle songs, and won a free dinner.

"Let me see the bill," he said, taking it from her hands. "How much tip you think I should leave?"

The waitress was embarrassed and nervous. "Four bits. That too much?"

Laura started to speak, but Pa's look silenced her. Pa put the bill on the table and reached into his pocket. "Here's two dollars for the meal and two dollars for the tip."

The waitress was clearly astonished. "But that's too—"

Pa smiled. "Buy some milk for your little ones. Come on, Laurie. Let's hit the road."

The rain had stopped, so they pulled the cover off the car. Laura drove to the edge of the road and stopped. "That was nice of you, Pa."

"What?" he said, trying to dry off his seat.

"Giving that waitress the money for the dinner you won."

Pa laughed. "I'd have paid twenty bucks for the memories I'm takin' with me."

They got back on the road and managed to get checked into the Joplin Hotel before it started pouring again.

"It's good to be back on the prairie again, ain't it, Laurie?" Pa said from the next bed.

Laura smiled in the darkness. "It's been different, Pa—that's all I can say."

"Good," Pa said, rolling over. "At least you ain't so much a stick-in-the-mud. I saw your feet dancin', Laurie; I saw 'em dancin'."

Laura fell asleep with a smile on her face and the memory of Fiddlin' Pa in her mind.

CHAPTER 23

MAD AS A HORNET

Rollo couldn't sleep. All the other parish kids were snuggled into their bedrolls spread across the floor, but he couldn't sleep. He was hungry. His stomach was growling. He had a headache. All he could think about was *food*.

The giant Mexican jumping bean kept buzzing in the box next to his head. "Wonder if you can eat a Mexican jumpin' bean?" he wondered to himself.

Carefully taking out the lacquered hornet's nest that he thought was a Mexican jumping bean, Rollo shook it back and forth.

Buzz-zz!

He put his ear to it.

Buzz-zz-zz!

He smelled it.

Buzz-zz-zz-zz!

He licked it.

Buzz-zz-zz-zz-zz!

And then, looking around to make sure no one was watching so he wouldn't have to share his bean delight with anyone, Rollo opened his mouth wide, wider. . . .

He bit into it with a loud crunch.

Buzz-zz-zz-zz-zz!
Hornets were flying everywhere!
Richie looked up, rubbing his eyes. "What's that sound?" He saw Rollo with the nest in his hand and hornets flying around his head.

Rollo shouted, "Help!" and tossed Richie the nest.

Richie screamed, "No—not to me!"

Now the other kids were waking up, trying to figure out what all the confusion was about. Richie tossed the nest to Burpo, who tossed it to the parish girls in the corner.

Father Walsh was awakened by all the screaming and ran into the parish room. Before he could say a word, the nest was tossed to him, and he was knocked over by all the children trying to get away from the hornets.

Rollo went running from the room with a dozen hornets in his pants, then stopped and dropped up and down on his rump trying to kill them.

Finally, Richie came running up, grabbed the hornet's nest from Father Walsh's arms, ran to the open window, and tossed it as far as he could.

A stream of hornets followed the nest, and as the sound of the hornets faded away, it was replaced by the wails and moans of the parish kids rubbing their hornet stings.

Father Walsh looked as mad as a hornet. "How'd these hornets get in here?" he asked, gingerly touching the hornet stings on his face.

Richie fingered a bite on his arm and shook his head. "Haven't got the foggiest idea, Father."

While the rest of the kids were putting baking soda on their stings, Richie gathered the Tigers around him. "Those hicks got us good—they got the Monroe Street Tigers."

He looked into each Tiger's eyes. "Are we gonna take that?"

"No way," babbled Rollo, his mouth swollen shut from stings. "We don't get mad, we . . ."

All the tigers grabbed hands in the center and shouted, *"We get even!"*

The next morning, Maurice pushed the Younguns forward. "Go on now. Do what you said you'd do."

Terry shook his head no, and Sherry clung on to Maurice's legs. "Don't let 'em hit me, Mr. Springer," she pleaded.

"Ain't no one gonna hit you, 'cept maybe your pappa when he finds out what you kids did."

"You gonna tell him?" Terry asked, a worried look in his eyes.

"That's between you and your conscience." Maurice patted Larry on the back and said quietly, "Go on, son. You're the oldest. You gotta do what you said you'd do."

Larry gulped and looked at the Monroe Street Parish kids staring at him. They were covered with patches of baking soda on their faces, arms, and legs.

Father Walsh had a bandage on his nose where a hornet had stung him. Richie had baking soda all over his arms. Burpo's right ear had swollen to twice its normal size.

Rollo had a pillow strapped to his fanny. "He ain't got nothin' to say that I want to hear."

Father Walsh raised his palms for silence. "Children, to forgive is the Christian thing to do. We must forgive those who trespass against us."

"Yeah, *right!*" mumbled Richie.

Father Walsh shook his head. "I'm sure these Youngun children didn't mean . . ."

"Phooey!" Burpo shouted.

"I'd rather shake with a snake," Richie said in a deep, low voice.

Things were getting out of hand, but Maurice didn't know what to do. After he'd gotten the story about what had happened on his farm—about the "Missouri raisins" and the "Missouri road apples," the meadow muffin, and the zebra—and *then* heard about the "giant Mexican jumping bean" that Rollo bit into—it was all he could do to not whale the tar out of the Younguns himself!

So he'd made them come to the parish hall to apologize and ask for forgiveness. The Younguns would rather have taken their chances with a nest of hornets than apologize to the kids who had called them hicks and hayseeds.

"I'll never sing 'Old MacDonald' again," said Burpo.

Father Walsh scolded the parish children, "Quiet! Listen to what this young man has to say."

All eyes were on Larry, especially Annabell's. For some reason spared from getting stung by the hornets, she giggled and winked at Larry, which made him all the more uncomfortable.

"Ah . . . I . . . we . . . want to apologize for what we done. It weren't right. We was mad for bein' called hicks and wanted to teach you a lesson, but that weren't the way to do it."

Richie pushed forward toward Larry, raising his fists. "You want us to accept his so-called *apology?*"

Father Walsh stepped between them. "I said, there'll be no fighting! We're going to settle this like Christians."

Richie looked into Larry's eyes and nodded his head, mouthing, "I'll get you."

Behind Richie, Annabell was winking at Larry, mouthing the words, *"You're cute."* Larry was clearly caught in a crossfire and could do nothing but blush.

Burpo asked loudly, "How do we settle things without punchin' their lights out?"

Father Walsh sighed. "If you were Notre Dame and Harvard, it'd be easy. We could—" He paused as an idea began to jell. "Why don't you kids play a friendly game of football together?"

"Do *what?*" asked Richie.

Father Walsh smiled. "Play football! City against country. Now, that would be a good American way to settle things and shake hands! Is that all right with you boys?" Father Walsh asked, looking around.

Richie rubbed his hands together, *"Certainly,* Father, *certainly.* The Monroe Street Tigers are ready to play *any time."*

"And you, Mr. Larry Youngun, do you think you and your friends are up to a game of football with these Monroe Street boys? I must warn you, I hear they're mighty good."

"They got equipment?" Richie sneered.

Maurice saw that Larry was struggling to say something, so he stepped in. "Certainly these boys have equipment. Why, our football team's known far and wide as the Mansfield . . . as the Mansfield . . ."

Maurice was struggling for words, but Sherry had a question that couldn't wait.

She tugged on Maurice's sleeve and asked, "What's the day that Cupid shoots his arrows?"

"Not now, child," he whispered.

"What's the name of their team?" Burpo asked, burping loudly. Father Walsh glared at him, so he looked down. "Excuse me, Father."

Sherry kept tugging. "Mr. Springer, what's the day that Cupid shoots his arrows?"

Maurice was flustered and confused, with everyone looking

at him and asking questions at the same time. He turned to Sherry. "It's Valentine's."

Richie guffawed. *"Valentines!* They call themselves the Mansfield *Valentines?"*

"The Tigers will murderize 'em," grinned Rollo.

Laughter spread through the parish children as fast as the blushes spread across Larry and Terry's faces.

"The *what?"* whispered Larry.

Richie smiled. "The Mansfield Valentines. Yes sir, I bet Cupid's sweeties sure know how to play this . . ." Richie paused and began prancing around the room like a cheerleader, "this *rough, tough* game."

Father Walsh clapped. "Then that settles it! And in honor of our local team, we'll have the game on Valentine's Day, which is the day before the parish kids return to St. Louis."

The Younguns were speechless. Larry felt humiliated. Annabell held her hand over her mouth, looking at Larry and giggling.

As Father Walsh loaded the parish kids onto the wagon for a trip through the country, Larry stood there glumly. He looked at Maurice. "Why'd you call us the Valentines?"

Maurice just shrugged. "I just got flustered when little sister asked me 'bout Cupid's day and . . ."

"You could have said *anything,* besides that," Larry moaned. "You could have called us the Mansfield Maulers or the Maneaters or the Mansfield Meanies. Even bein' called hicks or hayseeds would have been better than bein' called *Valentines."*

"We'll have a tough time playing when we feel stupid," Terry said, looking down at his feet.

Larry tugged at Maurice's sleeve. "We don't even know how to play football. Missouri Poole was tryin' to teach it to us last

week, but I got confused about what the nickelback does
and—"

"That's quarterback," Maurice corrected.

"And I don't understand nothin' 'bout wide deceiver or—"

"That's wide receiver," Maurice corrected.

"Can girls play?" Sherry asked. "I'd make a good Valentine."

"Yes, you would, child," Maurice said, scooping her up into
his arms. "You can be *my* Valentine."

"We don't know the rules of the game," Larry shrugged.

Maurice shook his head without sympathy. "Then you better
learn, 'cause those city boys want to sting your bottoms bad."

"But . . . but—" stammered Larry.

"But nothin'!" Maurice said. "Gettin' knocked on your butt
in football is better than lettin' those city boys kick it across
Main Street." Maurice walked off in a huff. "Bee stings, zebras,
rabbit raisins, road apples. You're all lucky they didn't string
you up."

Terry saw the mean eyes of Burpo and Richie and shook his
head. "We're in trouble now. Oh, man, what are we goin' to
do?"

Maurice heard him and spun around. "You're gonna play
football! Settle your differences the American way!"

CHAPTER 24

CAPE GIRARDEAU

Rev. Youngun looked out from the second-floor balcony of the Glenn House, where he was staying in Cape Girardeau. His church business was over, and he was worried about what to do next.

In his mind he went over the events since he arrived by train. Carla Pobst met him at the station, gave him a buggy ride around the Mississippi port, and took him to a restaurant on Water Street where the riverboat captains ate.

On the second day, after he finished with his church meeting, they even held hands and acted like teenagers while they strolled through the rose gardens around city hall. He felt awkward and exhilarated at the same time.

It seemed that the more he talked, the more he talked about his three children. After a while, Carla laughed, "Oh, Thomas, you don't have to sell me on your children. Let's talk about something else."

On the third day, he asked if she had settled up all her affairs and sold the estate, but all she said was that she needed a little while longer. She didn't know when she'd be moving to Mansfield, or even if she'd be moving anytime soon.

So they took another walk that afternoon just to be together, and as she'd put it, "not rush things," to let what would happen, happen. She said, "We've both lost someone we loved and have plenty of time to think our decisions over. We owe it to them."

He saw a tear come to her eye, but she laughed it away, squeezing his hand. "Look, Thomas!" She pointed from the bluff above the river. "Over there's Fort D from the Civil War, and that building down on Water Street—right down there— that's where General Grant made his headquarters when he was here in Cape."

She squeezed his hand harder and walked on. "And somewhere over there is where the Cherokee Indians crossed the Mississippi in 1838 on their forced migration from Georgia to Oklahoma. The Indians called it the Trail of Tears."

Rev. Youngun would remember that moment forever. She spun back around and kissed him. He hesitated, then melted into the warmth of her embrace, almost squeezing the life out of her, trying to keep her there forever.

"Oh, Thomas, I'm sorry. I just got carried away. Please, don't think badly of me," she pleaded, walking briskly toward her buggy.

The kiss had stopped just as suddenly as it came, and now he had only the memory of it in his mind, along with the memory of Norma and his children.

That evening he found himself walking the path where they'd kissed. Life was complicated enough for him without his falling in love with someone.

What am I goin' to do? he wondered, looking out on the quiet river town.

CHAPTER 25

TRAIL SIGNS

By midday, Laura and Pa were nearing Independence, Kansas, when the engine overheated.

"Oh, shoot!" Pa shouted. "We're just a few miles from findin' the old place. Why'd it have to go and break down now?"

Steam poured out from under the hood, so Laura pulled over in front of a blacksmith shop up ahead. Pa jumped out as the car came to a noisy halt.

"Don't lift the hood!" Laura warned. "Manly says to always let it cool down."

Pa shook his head. "Manly says too much." With a cloth he unlatched the lid and opened the hood. Steam engulfed him, knocking him back. "Now I know how a fish feels as he's joinin' the stew," Pa coughed, wiping his face.

He noticed the blacksmith with his long apron, watching from the double doors to his buggy shop. "Can you help us?" Pa asked.

The blacksmith stepped forward. "You folks got a problem?"

Pa rolled his eyes. "No, we're just lookin' for some weenies to roast in this steam heat." The engine shuddered, interrupting him. "'Course we got troubles! Can you help us?"

"Let's see. What kind of motor car is this, a Buick?" The blacksmith pulled a plug of tobacco and chewed down on it.

Pa was getting irritated and asked, "Can you help us?" The blacksmith kept chewing. Pa asked again, "I asked you a question—can you help us?"

The blacksmith finally said, "I know 'nough about motor cars to get by. Might take me a day or two, but . . ."

Pa shouted to the sky, "We're so close to findin' our house."

Laura sighed. "Mr. Blacksmith, can you—"

"Name's Lincoln. Lincoln Wyles."

Laura nodded. "Pleased to meet you, Mr. Wyles, but I need to know if you can fix my car."

"Maybe. Maybe not. Depends."

Pa was exasperated. "Depends on what?"

"Depends on whether I can fix it or not. Simple as that."

Laura stepped down. "Mr. Wyles, please try to fix our motor car. We'll wait under that shade tree while you look at it."

"I'll do my best—you can bet on it," the blacksmith said, then went and picked up his toolbox.

Laura pulled Pa toward the tree, but he struggled every inch of the way. "Let me go! I say, *let me go!*"

The blacksmith howled with laughter as Pa pulled to get free. Laura let his arm loose, and he snatched it away, trying to regain some of his dignity. "You embarrassed your Pa, pullin' me 'round like I was some kind of senile ol' coot!"

She started to speak, but Pa doubled over in pain. "Pa! Are you all right? Pa!"

"Help me down," he wheezed, reaching into his pocket for his pills. "Get me some water—quick!"

The pill burned under his tongue, but Laura rushed back with the water, holding the ladle and bucket in front of him. The blacksmith stood back, shaking his head.

"What's wrong with the old man?"

"Just having heart pains," Laura answered. "Pa, are you all right?"

Pa breathed deeply, waiting for the pill to take effect. Finally, he felt his strength returning. "I'm okay. It'll be all right in a minute."

Pa relaxed for a bit. Then he noticed something in the barn and stood up, walking away from Laura without saying a word. Inside, covered with dust and cobwebs, was an old covered wagon. He pushed against its springs, kicked at the wheels, and jumped up onto the seat.

Laura looked in. "Come on, Pa. You better sit under the tree and rest."

"Look at this wagon! Just like the one that carried us 'cross the prairie."

The blacksmith came in. "That's a real pioneer wagon, you know it?"

Pa ignored his comment. "You got any horses for this old covered wagon?"

"You bet I do! Best in the county," the blacksmith said.

Pa jumped down, dusting himself off. "You sure talk a lot 'bout bettin'."

The blacksmith smiled. "'Fore I changed my ways, used to be known as quite a gamblin' man."

"You got a team of four horses that we could rent along with that wagon while you be doin' your smithy work on our car?"

"Told you I do," the blacksmith grunted.

Laura spoke up. "Pa, we can wait until he fixes the car."

"Hold on, Laura." He turned to the blacksmith. "Now, since you got a wagon and a team of horses you ain't usin', why don't you rent 'em to us for a few days?"

The blacksmith scratched his chin. "Can't."

"Why *can't* you?" Pa said in a deep voice.

"What if you don't come back?"

"You'll have our car! Why, it's worth more than this wagon and its horses combined!"

"Ain't worth nothin', broke like it is."

Laura started to speak, but Pa raised his hand for quiet. "Tell you what, how 'bout you and me flippin' a coin? Heads you rent 'em to us for two–three days. Tails, you fix our car and we'll hang out at the hotel for a few days like a couple of lame 'possums."

"Don't gamble no more," the blacksmith snorted.

"This ain't gamblin'!" Pa exclaimed. "You can't really lose. You'll get paid for fixin' our car, either way, and you might just get some rent for that old wagon that's moldin' away."

Looking at the cobweb-filled wagon, the blacksmith turned and nodded. "Okay, just one flip."

Pa pulled out his lucky gold coin and rolled it around on his fingers. After a moment, he stopped and balanced it on his right thumbnail. "Just one flip is all it'll take, my good man. Just one flip like this!"

The coin went turning up into the air, right through the cobwebs on the ceiling. For a moment it was lost in the swirling dust dancing in the sunlight, but then it fell, glittering, back into view.

Pa slapped it onto the top of his left hand and lifted up his right palm. "Heads it is! Now, let's see those horses. Laurie," he said, turning to his daughter, "let's get this wagon cleaned up and move our things over."

Laura shook her head, grinning at her father. He was back in command, ready to lead them across the prairie.

When everything was packed, Pa climbed onto the wagon

and pulled Laura up. He took the reins and grinned at her. "Ready to hit the trail?"

She laughed. "Somehow I knew you'd get your way."

The blacksmith watched, shaking his head. "Make sure you come back."

Pa grinned. "Don't bet on everything. Where we're goin' is a lifetime away." Before the blacksmith could answer, Pa clicked the reins and the horses pulled the wagon forward.

Two people in a motor car tooted their horn and waved. Laura laughed. "They probably think we're part of the Will Rogers show."

Pa grinned. "Who cares what they think? We got ourselves a wagon. We got ourselves a covered wagon!"

The blacksmith walked up. "Say, where you goin', anyway?"

Pa stood up in the wagon and pulled up on the reins. "Why, we're goin' home. Home to the prairie!" He reached into his jacket pocket and pulled out his old, folded trail map. "Say, do you know the way to Indian Territory?"

"Indian Territory? Why, there ain't been no such thing since . . ."

Pa cracked the whip. "Since they chased us out." He cracked the whip again, and the horses jolted forward. "Move it, girls. Wagon forward. We're almost home."

The blacksmith shook his head as they pulled down the street between the honking cars. He muttered to himself, "Bet I don't see that wagon again—Bet I don't."

After several hours of bumpy traveling, Pa didn't want to admit he was lost, but nothing on his map seemed to be right. The roads went different directions, the creeks had new names, and the rock piles that had marked the trail were long gone.

"Look at them vultures," Pa said, pointing to three of them circling overhead.

"Just hope they're not waiting for us." Laura smiled, trying to lighten up the day.

"I just don't know where we are," he sighed, stopping the wagon on the edge of the two-lane road.

"Well, you know we're in Kansas and near Oklahoma." From behind them a motor car horn tooted ten times. "Move it! Move your wagon, you hicks!"

Pa put down the map and looked at Laura. "Did you hear what that fool called us?"

Laura sighed. "Pa, no one goes around in a covered wagon anymore. They just . . ."

Pa interrupted her. "They just don't have any manners." From behind them a car horn honked a half-dozen times again. Pa looked around the edge of the wagon and saw a young man honking the horn of his new Packard. A blonde with a feather hat sat next to him.

Seeing Pa's face, the man squeezed the bulb horn attached to his steering wheel. "Move it, Grandpa! Move over for progress, you old coot!"

The woman's laughter carried to them as Pa turned to Laura. "I don't like what that man's sayin' to us." Handing the reins to Laura, he stepped off the wagon.

"What are you going to do?"

Pa shook his head. "Teach this overgrown kid a thing or two 'bout manners."

Laura tried to protest, but Pa walked back to the car and unlatched the hood. The young man looked up. "Hey! Hey! What are you doin'?"

Pa looked over the hood and smiled. "Just givin' you a little help." He looked at the plugs and smiled when the first one he pulled out made the car sputter. The driver started screaming, but Pa just kept pulling plugs until the car conked out in one big shudder.

The young man was standing up in his car, trying to see Pa. His mouth was hanging open when Pa slammed the hood down. "What'd you do to my car?"

Pa shook his head. "First of all, your momma would be ashamed of the way you're actin'. Secondly, you ain't got no manners and no right to be callin' people names. And third," he paused, "I just don't like you or your car."

The man grabbed the squeeze-bulb horn from the steering column and began honking it loudly. "Hey, you! Hey, Old-Timer. Come back here! Fix my car!" When Pa turned and winked, the man was flabbergasted. "I'm warnin' you, I'm goin' to call the police!"

Pa stepped up onto the wagon ledge, turned, and laughed. "First of all, ain't no phone 'round here for miles. And if you do find one, I suggest you call a blacksmith to come fix your motor car." Pa wiped his brow.

He took the reins from Laura and cracked his whip for the horses to move on. The man kept screaming until they couldn't hear him anymore.

"What happened back there, Pa?" Laura was almost afraid to ask.

Pa shrugged. "Sometimes you just got to pull the plug to get some attention. He just needed remindin' of his manners, that's all."

After another hour of riding, Pa stopped again. "That's enough!"

Laura was surprised, "You want to go back?"

"No, not go back. Well, yes, I do."

Laura was confused. "I'm not sure what you're saying."

Pa picked up the map and put his finger on the spot. "That's where our house should be, and this is where we are," he said, pointing to another spot.

Laura looked up ahead. "But the road we're on is going in a different direction."

Pa nodded. "I know. Ain't it the darndest thing? What'd they have to change the old trail for? There were good signs along the old trail—rock piles, crosses. Now we ain't got nothin' 'cept signs like that," he said, pointing his finger to a billboard:

EAT AT PIONEER JOE'S
AUTHENTIC PIONEER FOOD
AND SPAGHETTI

"Guess you'd call that a modern trail sign, Pa," Laura giggled.

Pa shook his head. "If'n I'd seen a sign like that back in seventy-two, we'd have probably ended up in Italy."

Laura laughed. "Come on. Let's hit the trail, Pa."

Pa's eyebrows raised as an idea came to him. "That's it!"

"What?"

"You said it, Laurie! Let's hit the old trail again."

"What old trail? Where?"

Pa looked at the map, then back toward a big tree on a knoll above them, standing out like a lonely soldier. Without answering her, Pa pulled off the road and stopped the wagon in front of a barbed-wire fence.

Reaching under the seat, he pulled out a set of wire cutters and jumped from the wagon.

"What are you doing, Pa?"

"What's it look like?" he grinned, cutting the top wire.

"It looks like you're cutting somebody's fence."

Pa laughed, snipping the second wire. "And it looks like you're right!"

"But that's not right!" Laura protested.

Pa snapped the third and last wire. "If we're goin' to find our old place, then we got to ride the old trail again."

"But this is private property. It belongs to somebody!"

Pa looked at the map again and back to the tree. "Hold on. We're gonna cross some private property to get *back on the trail again!*"

Laura tried to speak, but fell backward in her seat as Pa cracked the whip. The team of horses pulled forward, building up speed as they raced toward the tree with Pa cracking his whip.

As the tree loomed closer, Pa shouted out, "I know that's the tree. I just know it."

Laura held onto the seat. "Sit down, Pa! You're goin' to hurt yourself."

Pa just laughed and cracked the whip, singing out:

> Old Dan Tucker was a fine old man;
> He washed his face in the frying-pan,
> He combed his hair with a wagon wheel,
> And died of the toothache in his heel.

Laura held on, laughing, trying to sing along, watching the wind blow through his salt-and-pepper hair. She saw the strength of his arms, the freedom in his eyes. It was wonderful to be on the prairie again.

"Whoa, girls, bring it down, now," Pa shouted out to the team.

He brought the wagon to a stop under the lone tree and jumped off. Walking around it twice, he spotted something and

CHARLES
AND CAROLINE
INGALLS,
MARY AND LAURA,
1870

rubbed away some dirt. On the tree was a smooth spot with letters carved in it.

"Come here, Laura—look."

Laura got off and walked over. Pa was pointing to deep cuts, long browned by time:

Charles and Caroline Ingalls, Mary and Laura, 1870

"You remember me carvin' that in during our stop?"

Laura tried to remember. "I'm not sure, Pa."

"You were just a little thing, but this was where we stopped to make camp. The grass was so tall that it was over the heads of our oxen. You thought we were crossing the ocean and said that this tree was a lighthouse."

Laura began to remember her father's hands, carving the tree while she sat and watched. Behind them, her mother made lunch from the game Pa had shot.

"Think, Laurie," Pa said. "Wild animals were everywhere. They were livin' without bein' afraid. A little fawn and her mother were standin' by the tree when we arrived, and you fed them some corn. That mornin' we saw bears eating wild berries along the creek."

Laura blinked her eyes and looked at Pa. "Was there a rainbow that day?"

Pa closed his eyes, then opened them, smiling. "There was! You pointed to the horizon and said that was where the gold was, that was where we'd find our special place."

"Where's the house?" she asked quietly.

Pa pointed. "Our house is just out there. Just before the horizon is where we'll find it."

"The pot of gold at the end of the rainbow," Laura said, looking off across the prairie.

CHAPTER 26

SEALED WITH A KISS

The knock on the door was so soft that Rev. Youngun didn't hear it for a few moments. "Thomas, are you in there?" Carla asked softly from the hall.

Putting down his newspaper, Rev. Youngun straightened his shirt and opened the door. "Carla, what are you doing up here?" he asked, worried about how her coming into his room might look to others.

"I just wanted to tell you that . . . that . . . that I was unable to sleep last night."

"What's wrong?"

"Oh, Thomas," she smiled, kissing him lightly on the lips. "I was thinking about you, about us."

"So was I," he blushed.

"What are we going to do?" she asked, hugging him.

"I know that I wish you were with me forever, but you said to let things happen."

Carla took him by the hand. "Come on, let's go for a walk."

Slipping out of the room without anyone's noticing, they headed down to the riverfront of town. It was a beautiful day with boats plying their trade up and down the Mississippi.

Stopping on the bluff above the town, Carla looked into Thomas's eyes. "There's something we've got to talk about."

"And what's that?" he asked, hesitantly.

"Children."

Thinking she was referring to his three, he said, "Three are a lot to handle."

"Yes they are, but that's how many I want. I thought about having six, but that's too many to love and . . ."

"But I've only got three, so you don't have anything to worry about."

"Thomas," she said, "I know you have three wonderful children. I mean that I want to have three babies. Three babies of my own."

Stunned, Rev. Youngun turned and looked out across the muddy river. "Three more babies," he mused, thinking what life would be like if he had three more Terrys.

"Yes," she smiled, squeezing his hand, "I'd like three girls. Three little girls I could dress up and spoil. Just give them all the things I never had when I was growing up. That's what we wanted, three little girls."

"We?" Rev. Youngun asked.

"Oh, I'm sorry. I was thinking about what my late husband and I talked about."

It was an awkward moment, but Rev. Youngun nodded. "I understand. Norma wanted to have a house full of kids. Would have had 'em too if the fever hadn't taken her."

Carla leaned over and kissed him on the cheek. "We can't change what's happened in our lives, and we can't dwell on it. What's happened is over. Life has to go on."

"You can still have those little girls," he said softly.

"But who am I going to marry?" she asked mischievously.

"You have someone else who comes halfway across the state to see you?"

"Not halfway across the state. Maybe across town, but . . ." she teased.

Rev. Youngun pulled away. "If there's someone else, just tell me now so I won't make a fool of myself."

Carla hugged him tightly. "Silly, there's just you. Thomas Youngun. You're the only one I think about."

"Then think about marrying me, Carla. Think about it real hard. 'Cause that's what I think I want to do."

"Think?" she smiled.

"I'd marry you right now, but I want to make sure that it's what we both want."

"And what about my three girls?"

"That's all right by me."

"Good," she smiled. "Let's seal it with a kiss."

"Seal what?"

"Silly, seal the fact that I think we're going to get married before this year is out."

"But . . ."

"No buts, Thomas Youngun, kiss me."

They sealed their feelings, hopes, and dreams with a long, slow kiss standing on the bank of the Mississippi.

CHAPTER 27

PRACTICE MAKES PERFECT?

"You're pathetic!" Beezer the parrot screamed from Uncle Cletus's shoulder.

Larry put the ball down and looked at the team. "He's right. We're pretty pathetic."

The Mansfield Valentines were a sight to see. Little James, Sweet, Li, Frenchie, Terry, and Sherry weren't much of a team. They'd been practicing for several days, but they only seemed to get worse.

Red Shaughnessy and the Irish boys from the Hardacres wanted to play, but not on the Methodist team. "I'd play, but my dad would tan my hide," said Red, shaking his head.

Larry sat down in the middle of the cow pasture. "We're gonna lose. They're gonna kick our behinds from here to St. Louie."

Watching from the side, sitting on hay bales, were various Mansfield kids. A half-dozen of them had stocking caps pulled down over their ears to hide their shaved heads. Head lice were still spreading around Mansfield.

On the other side of the field, standing with one crutch, was Johnny Scales. He wanted to play, but Larry was worried that he would get hurt. But he'd been coming every day to watch silently from the side.

Maggot came running across the field. "Hey, guys, I spied on 'em! Hey, guys, I saw 'em playin'!"

He stopped in front of them, so out of breath that Larry said, "Slow down, Maggot. Start from the beginnin'."

Maggot breathed deeply, then began scratching his head for no reason. Watching him scratch made the players feel so uncomfortable that they all began to scratch. "I seen 'em playin' over by the Catholic church. They play rough and tough. Father Walsh is coachin' 'em."

"What else did you see, Maggot?"

Maggot shook his head. "They got helmets and matchin' shirts and knee pads."

Sweet looked around. "We got equipment, too, don't we?"

"All we got is a ball," Larry said, looking down.

"Say your prayers!" shouted Beezer.

Terry shrugged. "Let's go see 'em play."

"Yeah," said Li. "I bet they ain't as tough as Maggot thinks."

So the Mansfield Valentines, led by the Younguns, sneaked across town and hid behind the ring of trees around the parish's clearing. Below them, the Monroe Street Tigers were playing real football—snapping the ball, running patterns, playing formations.

"They know the game," said Larry, shaking his head.

"I think we should just give up now and move to Alaska," moaned Sweet, watching Richie tackle Rollo in a flying leap.

Larry saw Annabell clapping for Richie's tackle. "All we need is practice. Practice makes perfect."

"You're kiddin' yourself," said Terry.

"Come on, guys," Larry said, "let's go back and practice some more."

"What's Mr. Springer doin' down there?" Terry asked, pointing to the side of the field.

"Hope he ain't coachin' 'em, too," moaned Li.

"If he is, he is. But I don't think he is. Come on guys, let's go," said Larry, walking away.

The Valentines started back to their cow pasture. Sweet tapped Terry. "Got any more of that ABC gum?"

Terry shrugged, "Maybe. Got any money?"

Sweet pulled out a shiny penny and smiled. "Got a penny!"

Terry looked at the penny and stopped chewing. "You run up ahead, and I'll go through my pockets and find you some."

"It's a deal," Sweet said, taking off. Terry pulled the gum from his mouth and flattened it into the gum wrapper he'd saved.

He raced ahead, "Hey, Sweet, I found some!"

Sweet eyed the wrapper with delight. "Give it to me!"

"Give me the penny first," Terry demanded.

Sweet handed him the penny and grabbed the gum, unwrapping it as fast as he could. "Whatflavorisit?" he mumbled, stuffing the gum into his mouth.

"It's new. Called Wrigley's Mystery Gum."

Sweet chewed some more. "No mystery to me. Tastes like onions . . . and pepper sausage . . . and garlic . . ."

Larry called, "Come on, Terry, let's go."

"Is that the mystery?" Sweet asked.

"I'm not sure," Terry smiled, "I found it a mystery that the gum tasted exactly like the onion, garlic, and sausage sandwich you had in your lunch box."

"Hey!" Sweet screamed out as Terry raced ahead. "You had no right to eat my sandwich!"

Maurice had watched the Younguns and their friends trying

to play football. Now he sat watching the Monroe Street Tigers *playing* football.

Father Walsh had noticed him sitting on a box, watching Richie pass the ball and walked over. "My team looks good. How's your team comin' along?"

Maurice was startled. "My team?"

Father Walsh winked. "I know you've been coachin' them. The way those kids look up to you, why, I bet you've got 'em playin' just like Notre Dame."

"They're comin' long just fine, Father, just fine."

Richie called a play, and the Tigers ran a perfect formation. "They look good, don't they?" Father Walsh said with pride.

"Lookin' good and winnin' are two different things," Maurice said, getting up to leave. "See you, Father."

Maurice walked back to where the Valentines were playing and stood next to Cletus, who still had Beezer on his shoulder.

"You're pathetic!" Beezer screamed as Sweet dropped another one of Larry's passes.

"I agree. I agree," Maurice mumbled to himself.

"Say . . . say . . . say what?" Cletus stuttered.

"Oh nothin'. Nothin' at all."

Larry saw Maurice watching and ran over. "Mr. Springer, do you know anythin' 'bout football?"

Maurice nodded. "I know how to play the game."

"We need a coach bad—I mean bad, Mr. Springer. Will you coach us?" Larry pleaded.

"Me? Coach? Well, I've never . . ."

Larry jumped up and down. "That's all right 'cause we've never played football, either. But if you'd coach us, we might have a chance."

The other players came running over, grabbing onto Maurice. "Please, Mr. Springer? Please?" they begged in unison.

Maurice sighed, looking at the motley team in front of him. They were all solemn, but as Maurice slowly broke a grin, first Sweet smiled, then Terry, then Li, then Frenchie, then Sherry, and finally Larry.

"Okay, okay," Maurice said, shaking his head. "I'll coach you on one condition."

"What's that?" Larry asked.

"That you got to do what I say."

"Okay!" they all shouted.

Maurice held up his hands. "And that means on and off the field. I don't want no more tricks or funny business played on those city boys, all right?"

They all nodded.

Li tugged at his sleeve. "We don't have any equipment? What are we goin' to do?"

Maurice shrugged. "I'll think of somethin'. Ol' Maurice will think of somethin'. *Now let's play football!"*

The children cheered and ran back onto the field. Maurice sighed, "I've got my work cut out now."

"Say your prayers," Beezer squawked.

"I am, I am," Maurice laughed.

For the next two days, Maurice worked the team into shape, teaching them how to hold the ball, run with it, catch it—all the basics. The plays he worked up were simple ones that they could all remember.

"Now remember," he said, pointing to Li, "when Sweet snaps the ball to Larry, you run right and Terry will run left."

"Got it, Coach," Li said. But no matter how many times Larry passed a perfect spiral, Li dropped it. Terry didn't just run a loop, he ran an entire figure eight, crashing into the other players.

Maurice took Larry to the side and looked at him. "Son, we

got ourselves a problem. You can pass the ball, but they can't catch it."

"What are we goin' to do?" Larry asked.

Maurice shrugged. "Maybe we ought to let Li or Sweet be quarterback. Can you catch?"

"Sure," Larry nodded.

"Let's see," Maurice said. "Run over toward the edge of the field."

Maurice watched as Larry got ten, then twenty, then finally forty yards out, and he passed the ball to him. The perfect spiral arched into the air. It was well beyond Larry, but he ran his heart out, diving at the last moment and catching the ball on the tips of his fingers.

Maurice was stunned. "That's it! That's the way!"

Every pass he threw, Larry caught. The last one Maurice threw way over his head, and it rolled down the hill into the pastures below. He stood with Larry on the edge of the field, looking down, trying to spot the ball.

Maurice sighed. "We might win the game, if we had a quarterback who could throw to you."

From below them came a voice. "Hey, Valentine, here's your ball." From sixty yards away, a perfect spiral shot into the air, dropping right into Larry's arms.

Maurice looked at the football and then to the pasture below. "That's our boy."

"That's no boy! That's Missouri Poole. She's a girl!" Larry said.

Maurice grinned, looking at Missouri, who was walking away. "Don't matter. That's our boy."

"Hey, Missouri," Maurice called out. "You wanna play on our team?"

"Larry's team?" she shouted back.

Maurice whispered, "Is she the one sweet on you?"

"Ah-huh," Larry said softly, looking down. "That's the one."

"Yes, on *handsome's* team," he called back, laughing.

"Stop that!" Larry protested.

"Hush!" Maurice snapped. He waved to Missouri. "Come on up here so we can talk."

"Be right there," she called back.

Johnny Scales limped up on his crutch and tapped Larry on the shoulder. "Larry, I want to play football."

"Johnny, I don't know."

Maurice answered, "You can play, Johnny. You can play second string." His heart melted as Johnny's face brightened.

"I can, Mr. Springer? You'll let *me* be on the team?"

"Certainly, child, certainly. Just 'cause you need a crutch to walk, don't mean you can't play the best you can play."

"Thanks, Mr. Springer," Johnny said, hobbling away.

Larry shook his head. "But he might get hurt!"

Maurice ruffled Larry's hair. "But if he don't try, his spirit might get hurt. Just 'cause someone's got a handicap don't mean he can't try his best and play."

Larry wasn't sure. "But—"

"No, son. Trust me on this one."

Maggot sneaked up and pulled on Maurice's sleeve. Maurice looked down and automatically started feeling itchy. "What you want, Martin?"

"Get outta here, Maggot!" Larry snapped.

"That's not nice," Maurice said, scolding Larry.

"I wanna be on the team, like Johnny," Maggot said.

"No . . . no . . ." Larry pleaded, tugging on Maurice's arm. "It's bad enough bein' called Valentines, but I don't want us bein' called maggots."

Maurice pulled his arm away. "His name's Martin Maggie,

not Maggot, and . . ." He raised his finger up to silence Larry, ". . . and he can be on our second string."

Putting his hands on Martin's shoulders, Maurice looked him in the eye. "Martin, you're gonna be a receiver when you play, and you're also going to be the fetcher."

Martin looked puzzled. "Is that like the catcher on a baseball team?"

"Naw. In football, the fetcher is a very important position. When I ask you to fetch water, you fetch the water, and when I ask you to fetch me somethin' to eat, you fetch me somethin' to eat. Okay?"

Maggot beamed. "Sounds great!" Then he had a puzzled look. "What we gonna do for equipment?"

"You all leave that to ol' Maurice. I'll figure somethin' out."

Missouri Poole came running up the hill and stopped in front of Larry, not winded at all. "Hi, Valentine." She winked. "Ready to kiss me yet?"

"Ain't you a bit young for smoochin'?" Maurice asked.

"Naw . . . since we're gonna get married in sixth grade, it ain't too early—right, Valentine?" she said, putting her arm around Larry.

Larry struggled to get free and thought of a plan. "Missouri, if you'll be the quarterback, I'll catch all your passes."

Missouri wiggled. "I like that! Catch this," she giggled, trying to kiss him on the ear.

Larry dropped to the ground. "I don't want you kissin' me."

"Then I won't play," Missouri said, picking up the football. "Hey, Johnny, catch this," she called out, passing the football in a high spiral that landed fifty yards down the field, at Johnny's feet.

Maurice was dumbfounded. "Girl, you can sure throw a football. No matter what it takes, you're goin' to be our quarterback."

"I want a kiss," she smiled, looking at Larry.

"No!" shouted Larry.

Missouri puckered up her lips toward Larry. "No!" he shouted.

"Then I'm not goin' to play!" Missouri said, stamping her foot.

Maurice was moving around, trying to think of what to do. "Larry will kiss you if we win the game. Is that a deal?"

Missouri looked at Larry and grinned. "If he'll give me a licorice kiss, then we've got ourselves a deal."

"No way!" Larry exclaimed, shaking his head at the thought of eating a long piece of string licorice with Missouri until their lips touched.

Maurice put his arm on Larry's shoulder. "Son, a kiss is a kiss." He looked at Missouri and nodded. "You got yourself a deal."

She looked at Larry and puckered her lips in and out. "Hot Lips Larry, you best get ready for my lips to kiss yours, 'cause we're gonna win that game."

She trotted off into the pasture, stopping to light her pipe. Larry shook his head.

"What's wrong?" laughed Maurice. "The odds are that those city boys are goin' to stomp you Valentines."

"I've heard of long shots comin' in," moaned Larry.

From across the other side of the field, a voice called out, "Hey, Valentine, how you doin'?"

Larry looked over and saw Annabell Davenport, who just happened to be taking a stroll by herself where Larry happened to be playing.

"Valentine?" Maurice laughed. "Ain't that one of them city boys' girlfriends?"

"She follows me everywhere. I don't know what's happenin'."

Maurice looked at the handsome boy and shook his head. "I think you've got yourself girl trouble. Yes, sir, you got yourself some girl trouble." "Come on, Valentine, let's go get somethin' to eat."

"No! I don't want any more hard-boiled eggs."

"You didn't let me finish. Eulla Mae's invited you Younguns to come over to our house for supper. She's got a surprise for you."

That evening, after a wonderful supper, Eulla Mae Springer brought out her surprise. She looked at the three Younguns and smiled. "Maurice told me how that other team has shirts with the team name on them, so . . ." she paused, reaching into her bag, "me and some of the ladies at the African Methodist Episcopal Church made some for you."

With a flourish, Eulla Mae pulled out a shirt that had a big, red heart on the front and back. Eulla Mae smiled with pride. "We made these special for your team, the Mansfield Valentines."

Maurice held his hand over his mouth to keep from laughing. Terry was in shock, and Larry was dumbfounded.

Only Sherry spoke. "I love 'em, Mrs. Springer. They're very pretty."

Terry whispered to Larry, "Those hearts are nothin' but bull's-eyes for the Tigers."

CHAPTER 28

THE PRAIRIE HOME

Pa pulled the wagon to a halt in front of a crumbled pile of rocks. "We're goin' the right way. Look here on the map. Here's the rock pile just inside Indian Territory."

Laura looked at the map and then back at the rock pile. "Seems to be in about the same area."

"We're on the right track. I told you we'd find some of my old trail signs. All I needed was to find that old carvin' tree. After that, we couldn't go wrong."

"I think we're lost, Pa."

"No we ain't," he said stubbornly. He examined the map again. "It was just fifteen miles from Independence . . . near Wayside and Niotaze . . . just west of Coffeyville and Jefferson and a bit north of Tyro and. . . ."

Pa looked around. The prairie had changed. There were trees where once there weren't. The land was fenced, and the creek was nowhere to be found.

"I didn't want to be too close to Fort Scott, 'cause of the Indians, and I didn't want to be on the road between Oswego and Chetopa."

"Why not?"

Pa shook his head. "Chetopa's town sign boasted that they

had the *best* billiard tables in southeastern Kansas. And Baxter Springs, why that was a wild man's place."

Laura laughed. "Was it that bad, Pa?"

"Bad? Why Baxter Springs was known as the town that grew so fast they forgot to build a church! They built a big brewery and sixty saloons and filled 'em with card tables." Pa laughed. "Ma thanked her lucky stars that we were a hundred miles from that town. Yes-sir-ree, the southeast corner of Kansas was the real Wild West in those days."

Laura shook her head. "Maybe we should turn around and go home, Pa. Maybe the Indians burned it down."

Pa rubbed his eyes. "It's gotta be right around here. I know it is . . . I just know it is."

Laura rested her head against his shoulder. "I believe you, Pa."

With a resigned grin and a shake of his head, Pa said, "Look at us. We're actin' like a couple of tinhorns." He jumped off the wagon. "Out here in the middle of prairieville, tryin' to follow a thirty-five-year-old map, stinkin' like skunks, lookin' for a house that we can't find. Why, people would think we're crazy if they saw us now."

"Maybe we are," she laughed.

Pa shook his head. "It's got to be around here someplace. Weren't no road, but I knew it when we found it." Pa smiled, deep in thought, pointing to the west. "I called out to your ma, "Here we are, Caroline. This is where we're gonna build our house!"

It was coming back to Laura. "I remember the big sky and the treetops peeking out from the creek bottom. Prairie chickens were running and hiding in the grass. Mary and I jumped off the wagon and chased them. You and Ma unloaded the wagon, and Ma made us beds under the wagon-cover tent you put up."

Pa took off his hat and wiped his brow. "I scratched out a place for our fire and went and got a load of logs in the wagon."

Laura nodded. "And when you came back, I pointed out the markings of an old trail leading off through the tall grass. You told me it was an Indian trail. I begged you to follow it and show me a papoose, but you told me that—"

Pa interrupted her. "—That Indians would only let you see them when they wanted you to."

Laura smiled. "That's okay, Pa. We tried."

Pa shook his head, looking around. "There just weren't these trees and bushes 'round here before. There should be a creek bottom just north of here, and over there were trees along the Verdigris."

"Let's take a walk, Pa. Okay?"

Pa helped Laura down, and they walked in the direction Pa thought the creek bottom was. The prairie was alive, hopping around them. A meadowlark skimmed along the grass. Dickcissels clung to the grass stalks, and grasshoppers scratched their legs like violins.

A pair of jackrabbits bounded past them, and gopher patterns criss-crossed the grass in front of them. Not more than a quarter mile away, they found a shallow creek trickling across the prairie, hidden by underbrush.

"Is this it, Pa?"

Taking off his hat, Pa looked around. "Yup, I think it is. Look at that!" he exclaimed, sliding down the bank. He hopped rocks, coming to the remnants of a stone dam. "I built this bathing hole for you."

Laura's eyes widened. "Is this where you used to bring me to wash?"

Pa nodded. "Same place. That means our place is just up over there," Pa said, pointing east.

They walked in silence, hearts pounding. Then Pa stopped. "Let's go get the wagon. It's only fittin' that we come back the same way we arrived."

He guided the wagon carefully through the trees and underbrush, watching for signs. The first one was the remains of a wooden fence. "This is it," Pa nodded.

"Are you sure?"

"'Course I'm sure. What other claim stakers would build a three-pole fence 'stead of a two-pole fence?"

At the edge of a clearing, they stopped. Pa looked nervous as he tied up the reins. He helped Laura down, and they both stood, wondering what they would find in the clearing.

Pa started to part the bushes, then stopped. "Can't," he said, shaking his head.

"Oh, Pa, come on," Laura said softly.

"You look," he said. "I've come this far. I don't want to be the one to see it, if it's changed."

"Oh, Pa," she said, suddenly feeling sorry for her father.

He turned around. "Maybe we should just go back now. Don't know if I want to see it, if it's not the same."

"This is silly. Just look, Pa. Just look."

He grabbed her hand gently. "You look first. Do it for your old Pa."

Laura took a deep breath and slowly parted the branches. She peered through the leaves and saw—nothing.

"What you see?" Pa asked nervously.

"I don't see a thing, Pa, except for some brush."

"Let me see!" Pa said, pushing the branches back.

He looked, then turned to Laura. "Where the heck is it? It was right there!" He looked again. "I built the place right there," he said, pointing toward the clearing. "I built it with my own hands. It was so big that we should have been able to see it from the distance!"

Laura grabbed his hand and pulled him along. "Come on, Pa. Let's see for ourselves." They walked slowly forward, holding hands.

"Here was the animal shed," he said, pointing to the remains of barely visible walls. "And over there should be the well I dug by hand. Almost killed myself and the neighbor who helped, diggin' it."

Laura walked to the spot and found the wooden top still sturdy on the well. "Here's a well."

"Look at the corner. See if it's got my initials, 'CI,' on the corner."

Laura wiped the dirt away and saw the initials carved into the wood. "Your initials are here, Pa." She stood up. "But where's the house?"

Pa pulled on Laura's arm, then stopped short. "Here it is—or was," he said, pointing down. In front of them was the post outline of their house. Pa walked it off, shaking his head.

"I remember it being so much bigger," he said sadly. "I thought it was almost a mansion."

Laura looked at how tiny—really tiny—their home on the prairie was and walked the perimeter of the twelve-by-fifteen-foot walls.

Pa sighed. "Either the place shrank, or it sure grew in my memory."

Laura smiled, feeling the same pain of finding that the remains were nothing like the homestead they wanted to believe existed. "I remember the door you were so proud of."

"It was right here." Pa pointed, pretending to open it. "I lathed it for days." He walked a few steps into the house. "We ate here," Pa said, pointing down, "right next to the chimney. Made the table and chairs myself, the hardwood floor. Your ma just had to have a hardwood floor."

"That was the floor we danced on," Laura said softly.

"It was the only handcut floor for twenty miles around!" Pa walked over to the corner. "And Ma and me slept here." He walked over to the opposite corner. "And you and your sister slept over here. And right here is where Dr. Tan saved you from the fever."

Laura walked over to her bedroom corner and closed her eyes. A smile came to her face as she remembered it all. She could remember the chill of the nights and the heat of summer days when the hawks screamed overhead, hunting for rabbits. She remembered Ma doing her laundry and reading the Bible to them.

She smiled at the thought of herself and Mary playing along the creek bottoms, watching for snakes and spying on deer, dipping their feet into the cool water of Walnut Creek, tossing leaf messages onto its bubbles, wondering if they would make it eastward past Onion Creek and then to the Verdigris and then to the Arkansas and finally to the mighty Mississippi.

It was all right in front of her. The house was alive again. She and Mary were sitting in the corner, looking at the newspaper pictures of fancy cassimeres, broadcloths, calicoes, and candy. Ma's favorite inscribed plate was on the mantel, above the Christmas stockings. Pa was young again, coming in from the fields with game he'd shot. Ma was in the corner, working on dinner. The rooms were aglow with love. It was everything she remembered, everything she wanted to find again.

"What you thinkin' 'bout, Laurie?" Pa asked softly. "It might have been small, but we made the best of it, didn't we?"

With her eyes still closed, Laura whispered, "I wanted to see it again, and I can see it now, Pa—I can!"

"Tell me—tell me what you see," Pa said softly, closing his eyes.

Laura wrapped her arms around herself. "I remember running happily through the fields, jumping into your arms, you spinning me around and around."

Pa joined in her memory and remembered that time when everything seemed so happy. He reached out in his mind and touched the cabin walls that he'd cut by hand, the tables and chairs that he'd carved as a special treat for Caroline, the real glass windows. He saw Caroline popping corn for the girls, singing a Christmas song. His rifle was hanging above the doorway, and the calico curtains separated the sleeping quarters.

It's all here again, he thought to himself, *just as I remembered it.*

Opening one eye, he saw that Laura was still wrapped in her memory, so he quietly walked back to the wagon.

In her mind, Laura was lying on the improvised bed, lost in the flickering firelight patterns on the walls. The warmth made her drowsy. She could hear her mother saying, *"Charles, get out your fiddle and play Laura to sleep."* Pa nodded and opened up his fiddle case and began playing softly. She could hear it.

When Laura opened her eyes, Pa was standing at the edge of the house's outline, playing softly, playing a special song.

He winked at Laura. "Maybe you really can't go home again, but that don't mean we can't keep our special dreams." He walked over and kissed her forehead. "The old home is alive and well up here," he said, tapping the side of his head with one finger.

"It's where it's always been," Laura whispered. Tears welled up in her eyes as Pa's head moved with the fiddle notes.

Pa dipped the fiddle. "It seems that life went from good to bad when we had to leave this place. I've spent half my life thinkin' about the what-if's, wonderin' if things would have ended up different if we'd been able to stay."

Laura shook her head sadly. "There's a plan and purpose for us all, Pa."

Pa stopped to wipe a tear from his eye. "It's just . . . it's just . . . I keep thinkin' how Freddie's life never had any joy in it."

"Oh, Pa, don't hurt yourself. Don't think about it."

"I have to. I *could* have played him a happy song just once. It wouldn't have taken no more than a minute of my time, but I was too stubborn." He stopped, trying to keep from sobbing.

Laura walked over and hugged him. "Play a song for him now, Pa."

Pa played his heart out to the ocean of prairie surrounding them, standing in the center of where the house had been, dipping the bow toward the ground then back toward the sky. The happiness of that time was alive again.

After the song, Laura put her arm on Pa's shoulder. "Come on, Pa. It's time I got home to Manly, and you got to go home to Ma."

Pa nodded and walked behind her, then stopped. "Wait a minute! I left somethin' back there."

Stepping quickly toward the house, he walked over to the remains of the fireplace and looked around, finally digging at a spot two hands' length from the back.

"What are you looking for?"

Pa dug a little deeper and pulled out a moldy old cloth-wrapped object. "This," he said. "I put this here when we were

forced out. Now it's time for you to take it home—to your home."

"What is it?" Laura asked.

Pulling off the cover, Pa dusted the dirt off a plate. He held it up for Laura to read.

Home is where the heart is.

Laura took it from his hands. "That's the plate Ma thought you lost."

"I told a fib. Didn't want to fib, but I knew she wouldn't let me leave her special plate. But I felt I was leavin' my heart and soul here, so I buried it. Swore I'd come back one day."

Laura pulled Pa to his feet. "You did come back. You kept your promise to yourself."

"I want you to have the plate, Laurie, 'cause after I'm gone, you'll be the one keepin' these memories alive."

Laura reached out and took it from his hands. "I'll take the plate with me, and I won't tell Ma your secret."

At the edge of the clearing, Pa and Laura turned to look back on the clearing one more time. Pa tipped his head and grinned at Laura. "At least we found it, didn't we, Laurie?"

She laughed and hugged him. "I think we found a lot of things on this trip."

He helped her back into the wagon, and as they rode off into the twilight, Pa sang out to the prairie:

> Oh, I am a gypsy king!
> I come and go as I please!
> I pull my old nightcap down,
> And take the world at my ease.

Laura laughed. "I never thought of you as a gypsy, Pa, but now that you mention it, you did kind of travel around like one."

"Maybe I am the gypsy king. Maybe I am."

Their voices drifted across the darkening prairie. "Now let's get on back home. Manly's waiting." Pa laughed, cracking the whip. "I've got an idea. Maybe we should try to find our house in the woods by Lake Pepin."

"No."

"Oh, Laurie, come on."

"No!"

CHAPTER 29

THE BIG GAME

The Mansfield Valentines were assembled behind a haystack on the side of the field. Shouts and jeers from the assembled crowd drifted over to them.

"You call this football equipment?" Sweet asked, trying to get the strange helmet on.

"Beggars can't be choosers," Maurice laughed. "Go on, put the stuff on. It'll work—trust me."

"I think you're trickin' us," Terry muttered, putting the rusting old miner's hat on his head.

"Where'd you get these things?" Little James asked.

"Found 'em at the dump 'bout two years back. Thought they'd come in handy one day—and they sure did!" Maurice exclaimed, admiring the team.

They were certainly a sight with their Valentine jerseys, milking pads for knee pads, and old farmer boots instead of football shoes.

Terry and Larry had miners' caps on; Little James, Frenchie, Maggot, and Johnny had rusty army helmets on; Sweet had a cooking pot on his head; Sherry had a hat with birds on it; and Missouri had a baseball cap.

"Mr. Springer, these pants are too big," Terry whined. They were three times his size.

"Just tie 'em up with this rope," Maurice said. "You'll be all right."

"This straw itches," complained Li, trying to push the stuffing away from his neck and onto the top of his shoulders.

"Who ever heard of straw for shoulder padding?" Little James moaned.

"You'll be glad you have it when the time comes," Maurice said.

"Let's play ball," Missouri shouted.

The team took a collective deep breath and ran toward the field. Missouri jogged next to Larry, puckering her lips. "Want to kiss me now . . . just a kick-off peck?"

"No, that's not the deal," he said, racing ahead.

From the stands he heard a wolf whistle, and he looked up. Annabell Davenport was winking and waving to him. Larry was so flustered that he ran right into the rest of his team, who were assembled on the field, listening to the referee.

The Monroe Street Tigers, resplendent in their fine new uniforms, laughed as the Valentines fell all over themselves. Along with the regular Tiger members, several other parish kids had joined to make up a full team.

Four-Eyes Johnson, the desk clerk of the Mansfield Hotel, was speaking to the teams. He got his nickname for the thick glasses he wore. He didn't see well, and Maurice thought he would make a good referee. He was blind as a bat.

Maurice was smiling from the side. He leaned over to Cletus, the combination scorekeeper/timekeeper, and laughed, "That Four-Eyes is the perfect ref for this game. Gives us an extra edge, don't it?"

"It . . . it . . . it . . . that's right. Smart thinking," stuttered Cletus. "Say," he tapped Maurice, "how . . . how . . . how . . . much is two plus two?"

Maurice rolled his eyes. "You'll do just fine, Cletus. I'll tell you what to write down."

"Say your prayers!" Beezer shouted to the Valentines.

Richie looked up at the squawking parrot and smiled at Rollo. "Even their parrot knows they're done for!"

"Yeah," snarled Burpo, "we'll murderize 'em." He tried to hold it back, but couldn't, and let out a loud belch.

Richie wiped his eyes. "I told you not to eat sardines before the game!"

"Sorry," Burpo blushed, letting out an almost silent second burp.

Cletus rang the bell. "Sixty . . . sixty . . . fifty seconds to game time."

Four-Eyes looked at the Monroe Street Tigers. "Okay, Valentines, you know the rules—"

Richie turned to Rollo. "Some ref. Hey, *we're* the Monroe Street Tigers—we ain't the sissy Valentines!"

Four-Eyes took off his glasses, "Er, sorry." He turned to the Valentines. "Okay, Valentines, you boys know the rules—"

Missouri interrupted him. "And us girls know the rules, too." Sherry nodded her head in agreement.

Maggot screamed from the side. "Come on, guys, you can beat 'em."

Johnny shouted out, "You can do it, Valentines."

Behind them, fifteen or so kids with stocking caps pulled down over their ears were sitting in the stands, scratching their heads with one hand and waving with the other.

Richie shivered, shaking his head. "Man, that's all we need to take home from the sticks—some lice."

Cletus rang the bell, and the coin was flipped to see who would kick off. The Tigers won the toss and elected to receive.

Sweet held the ball down, and Larry kicked it high in the air. "Good kick, Valentine," Missouri winked, running past him down the field.

From the first moment of the game, the Valentines were clearly outclassed. Richie took the kick and raced down the field, scoring a touchdown. Maurice shook his head. "This is going to be a *very* long game."

Near the end of the first half, the score was Tigers twenty-one, Valentines nothing. Four-Eyes had missed a dozen fouls that the Tigers had pulled, and Cletus was still calling out fourteen by the time the score had gotten to twenty-one.

Maggot came up and pulled on Maurice's sleeve. "Can I play now? Can I, coach?"

Maurice shook his head. "Ah . . . not now. Why don't you go check out their equipment during the break and see what they got?"

"Okay!" Maggot shouted, happy for an assignment.

Maurice took his dejected team behind the haystack to cheer them up. "It's only a game."

"No it ain't," said Missouri in a disgusted tone. "I want my kiss, so we gotta win." She turned and looked at Larry. "Are you throwin' the game on purpose?"

Larry shook his head, "Me? No, no way! I'm tryin'!"

Maurice raised his hands. "I think we need to start off the next half with the boo-boo-boy play, and then we'll roll into the Cupid play, all right?"

The bell was rung for the game to begin again. The Valentines all nodded their heads in agreement and raced back onto the field. Over on the other side, Maggot had finished trying on all the Tigers' helmets.

He walked back across the field, scratching his scalp. "Wonder if I have head lice?" he said to himself. He looked at the tips of his fingers. They were alive with little white crawling things.

"Better not let anyone wear my helmet," he told himself as he walked back to the Valentines' bench, "'cause that's how you spread head lice."

Richie stood on the side and looked at his team. "Okay, men, put on your helmets. Let's go for one hundred to nothin'!"

The Tigers were overconfident. When the Valentines received the kick, Larry did a hand-off to Missouri, and she took it to the twenty-yard line. In the huddle, Missouri called for the boo-boo-boy play.

In the Tiger huddle, Rollo and Burpo were scratching their heads. Richie frowned. "What's wrong?"

"Just itch, that's all," said Burpo.

When Frenchie snapped the ball, Larry stayed back to block while Terry and Little James went wide. Missouri did a hand-off to Larry, and at that instant, Terry and Little James did figure-eight maneuvers, then stopped in midfield, shaking around.

"What are they doin'?" Burpo asked.

Rollo scratched under his helmet. "Dancin', I think. I itch!"

While the Tigers were scratching and watching the shaking Valentines, Larry did an end run and scored a touchdown. Cletus rang the bell, shouting, "Tou . . . tou . . . *home run!*"

Maurice was jumping up and down and was beside himself when the Valentines intercepted Richie's pass to Burpo, who had stopped to scratch again.

Missouri called for the holy roller play, and when the ball was snapped, Sweet dropped to the ground like a cheese log and Larry and Terry rolled him into the Tigers.

In the confusion, Missouri tossed an easy pass to Little James, who scored a touchdown. Maurice jumped around, and

Cletus rang the bell, shouting, "Home run, home run! Twenty-one to four . . . four . . ."

"Fourteen! Twenty-one to fourteen!" Maurice shouted.

Richie couldn't get the Tigers to perform right because they were all scratching, but he managed to keep the Valentines from scoring for the rest of the third quarter.

Maurice thought they might be able to tie the game, and by the middle of the fourth quarter, he thought that it might just go their way.

Maggot tugged at his sleeve. "Can I play now? Can I coach?"

"How 'bout me, coach?" Johnny asked.

Maurice looked at the boys. He'd promised them they could play. At that moment Rollo threw a crushing block that took Frenchie and Li out of the action.

"Okay, boys, get on in there and play," Maurice ordered.

Maggot did his best, but he was knocked down on every play. Missouri tossed Johnny an easy one that he caught, but Burpo knocked him over with a crunch.

Richie walked over to help Burpo up and saw the pain that Johnny was in. He reached down and pulled Johnny up. "You all right, kid?"

"I'll be all right! I can play football as good as anybody."

"Sure you can—sure you can," Richie said softly, watching Johnny limp back to the huddle on his crutch. "That's a brave kid," he said to himself.

With just minutes to go, Sweet dropped an easy hand-off, and Richie ran with the ball. He was almost to the goal line when Larry tackled him.

"Not bad for a hayseed," Richie nodded.

Larry shrugged. "We try."

Burpo went wide for an easy pass and score, but he stopped

to scratch, and Terry dashed up and intercepted the ball. His pants were so big that he was holding them up with one hand.

He saw Rollo coming toward him, so he ran to the side and stuffed the ball into his pants. Rollo didn't see him behind the other players, so in the confusion over where the ball was, Terry skipped and did circles down the field to the goal line.

"Hey, Tigers, I've got the ball!" he shouted, sitting on it.

"Tie game! Tie game!" Maurice shouted.

"Si . . . si . . . fifty-five seconds to go," Cletus called out.

The Tigers huddled, and Richie whispered, "It's time for the St. Louie Special. Any questions about the play?"

Burpo gulped and belched out enough sardines and garlic to sink a ship. Richie gagged, and Rollo's eyes began to water.

"Dadgumm it, Burpo! If you gotta burp, burp on *them!*" he screamed, pointing to the Valentines.

"Sorry," Burpo said sheepishly. "I was hungry."

Rollo took the kick, but Burpo tripped Larry, and in the ensuing pileup, Sherry grabbed the ball.

Four-Eyes peered at her jersey. "What team you on?"

"Valentines." she giggled.

"Valentines' ball!" Four-eyes shouted.

"Do the Cupid play—now!" Maurice shouted.

"Do we gotta?" Larry shouted.

"Yeah! Now!" Maurice nodded from the side.

When the ball was snapped, Sherry took the hand-off and jumped into Larry's arms. Larry ran down the field with Missouri beside him to block. Every time someone got near him, Larry put Sherry on the ground, and she ran to Missouri, then back to Larry, until they were all tackled at the twenty-yard line.

In the huddle, Missouri looked at the team. "Okay, Larry,

you and Johnny go right for the pass, and, Maggot, you block from the center. Got it?"

The ball was snapped. Sweet did another holy roller, and Larry and Johnny went right. Missouri sent a perfect spiral toward them.

Johnny stopped next to Larry. "Take it, Larry! Win it for us!"

Cletus shouted out, "Twenty-one . . . one . . . nineteen seconds!"

"Say your prayers!" Beezer squawked.

Larry turned and shook his head. "You take it, Johnny. Win one for Mansfield."

The pass was coming right at them. Johnny planted his crutch firmly on the ground.

As the ball arched toward him, Maurice whispered, "Catch it, Johnny! Catch it."

Everyone in the stands was silent. Father Walsh muttered, "Go for it, boy."

Richie started across the field to tackle Johnny, but slowed to a crawl, watching the ball head toward the crippled boy. "Do it kid! Do it!" Richie whispered.

Johnny reached up and caught the ball. He couldn't believe it! *"I caught it, Larry! I caught it!"* he screamed, waving his crutch in the air.

Larry's eyes welled up. "You sure did, Johnny! *You did it!"*

Maurice shouted, "Don't just stand there—score!"

Richie started forward at a half-trot, but Larry saw the difference in his rival's eyes. When Richie got within earshot, Larry shook his head. "You're lettin' him score, ain't ya?" he said, watching Johnny hobble toward the goal.

"You and I'll play football again, but that kid needs to win today," Richie said.

Maggot came up, running into them both, sending them rolling onto the ground. The Mansfield crowd was cheering.

"We won!" Maurice shouted.

Johnny, holding onto the ball, leaned against the goal post, tears streaming down his face. Some of the local kids picked him up on their shoulders, carrying him across the field.

Larry reached out and shook Richie's hand. "I'm sorry for what we did at the farm. Weren't right. If you want to punch me, go ahead. I deserve it."

Richie gave him a soft punch that just grazed his chin. "There, that'll settle it. I shouldn't have called you a hick. That wasn't right, either."

"Come on, Larry. Let's celebrate," Sweet called out.

"See ya," said Larry.

"See you 'round like a donut," winked Richie.

"Hey, Richie," Burpo called out from the side, "Father Walsh thinks we all got head lice!"

Larry turned to see Missouri racing down the field with a long string of red licorice in her hand. "Time for my kiss, honey britches. Time to play kissy lips!"

"Oh, man, I gotta get outta here!" Larry shouted, racing across the field.

He managed to elude Missouri by jumping over the seats and benches, crawling behind the wagons, and finally jumping inside a haystack. Thinking he was finally safe, he lay back in the warm hay and took his hat off.

"Hi, Valentine," Annabell said, lifting the hay up and waving a small string of red licorice. "I've been waitin' for you."

Terry stuck his head into the haystack. "What's goin' on?"

"Let's get outta here!" Larry shouted, grabbing his hat and running from the haystack.

Annabell laughed and winked at Terry. "You're cute, Red."

Terry stuck his tongue out. "And you're cracked," he laughed, backing away. "Hey, Larry! Wait up!"

CHAPTER 30

GOOD-BYES

Rev. Youngun's train was arriving in Mansfield. It had been a quiet ride, except for the caged monkeys that the organ grinder was holding on his lap in the back of the car.

It seemed that half of Mansfield was gathered at the station. The Younguns were there to greet their father. Uncle Cletus was taking the train to St. Louis to catch a riverboat job, and was leaving Beezer with the children. The Monroe Street Tigers were taking the same train going home, and Pa was returning by train to De Smet.

"Why'd you have to shave our heads, Father Walsh?" Burpo asked, pulling his stocking cap down.

"That's the only way to really stop the fellas," Father Walsh said, pulling his own stocking cap down. "Still don't know how you boys got 'em. We were being so careful at the parish."

Larry snickered at the fifteen parish kids in stocking caps. Only Annabell didn't have one on. "I'd hate to have head lice," he said to Terry.

Uncle Cletus pulled his stocking cap down. "I wish I didn't get 'em."

"Oh, sure! Taco head!" Beezer screeched.

Terry reached up and scratched Beezer's head. They'd pulled

half his feathers out, trying to get the nits off his head. "I think Beezer needs a stocking cap."

Annabell came over to Larry and said. "I'm sorry, Larry. I . . . I wish we lived near each other."

Larry blushed. "Thanks, Annabell. So do I. I think you're cute."

The train came into the station and pulled to a stop. Larry turned. "I gotta go. My pa's come home. See ya."

"See ya, Valentine," Annabell sighed, shaking her head.

Rev. Youngun was the first off the train, and the three Younguns grabbed onto his legs. "Hold on, hold on. Let me show you the present I brought you."

Right behind him, the organ grinder was carrying his two caged monkeys. Terry looked at them, and his eyes went wide. "We don't want 'em! Send 'em back.!"

Rev. Youngun was perplexed. "What?" Then he saw the monkeys and burst out laughing, scooping Sherry and Terry into his arms. He got down and hugged Larry. "You three children are my whole life. You're the only monkeys I need!"

"You're pathetic!" Beezer screeched out, and they all laughed.

Laura, Manly, and Pa entered from the other side of the station.

Pa shivered. "Keep 'em away from me. I don't want no cooties on me!"

Manly laughed. "Pa, you're a character. You'll never change."

"Takes one to know one," Pa winked. He pointed to some men getting off the train, wearing clean-pressed, store-bought cowboy clothes. "Now those are *real sure-nuff* cowboys! he laughed.

"Just like your song, Pa," Laura smiled.

He kissed Laura on the cheek and held her arms. "Laurie, can't say we didn't try to go home again."

Laura hugged him. "No, Pa, we did go home again—and back. We found that home really *is* where the heart is."

She let go of Pa and hugged Manly. "And I've learned that my heart is at Apple Hill Farm—with the *other* man I love."

Pa nodded, tapping the side of his head. "Just remember, the good old days, the days of long ago, are just a memory away."

Pa's train was ready to leave, so he climbed aboard. As the train started to pull forward, he took the gold coin from his pocket and flipped it in the air. "Call it, Laurie! Call it."

Laurie watched the coin turn over and over. She shouted, "Heads!" and caught it with one hand, slapping it down on her palm the way she'd seen Pa do it.

The train was pulling forward, and Pa nodded. "Heads, ain't it?"

"Yes," she nodded. Wide-eyed. "How'd you know?"

Pa smiled. "I'm passin' my luck on to you, Laurie. Remember, luck is what you make of it."

Laura turned the coin over in her hand and saw it was a double-headed coin. *You old rascal,* she laughed to herself.

Pa laughed. "I never believed in gamblin'," he called out. "Remember to always play heads up and stand strong for what you believe."

Laura looked at the coin again, and heard Pa's sweet fiddle notes playing out "City Cowboy." He was standing on the back of the train, playing to the world with a smile. Laura waved and shook her head. Pa was Pa. There was no one in the world like him.

As the train pulled down the tracks, Manly put his arm around Laura and hugged her. "I missed you, honey. I really missed you."

"I missed you, too," she said, nuzzling into his chest.

"Let's go home and get *reacquainted*," he whispered.

Laura took the coin out and said, "I'll flip you for it." She flicked her thumb, sending the coin up into the air. "I'll call it!"

Manly interrupted her. "No, *I'll* call it." He watched the coin flip over and over. "Heads," he said, winking at her.

Manly caught the coin in the air and slapped it on top of his palm. He slowly raised his hand, then smiled. "Heads it is." Manly chuckled. "Your pa showed me the coin this mornin'. Told me you'd try to pull a fast one on me as soon as he gave it to you."

Across the platform, Sweet called out to Terry, "Got any more of that ABC gum?"

Burpo walked over to Terry and tapped him on the shoulder. "You got some of that ABC gum for me?"

Terry smiled. "Sure," he said, pulling some out of his pocket. "Hope you like it."

Burpo opened the packet and stuffed the soft gum into his mouth. "You're all right, Youngun. Thanks for the gum."

Terry shrugged. "Anythin' for a friend, friend."

Burpo chewed some more, trying to figure out the flavor. "Strange taste. Have you tasted it yet?"

Terry winked and skipped away. "You might say I've already tried it!"

ABOUT THE AUTHOR

T. L. Tedrow is a bestselling author, screenwriter, and film producer. His books include the eight-book "Days of Laura Ingalls Wilder Series": *Missouri Homestead, Children of Promise, Good Neighbors, Home to the Prairie, The World's Fair, Mountain Miracle, The Great Debate,* and *Land of Promise,* which are the basis of a new television series. His four-book series on The Younguns, to be released in 1993, has also been sold as a television series.

His first bestseller, *Death at Chappaquiddick,* was made into a feature film, for which he wrote the screenplay. Tedrow's screen credits include co-producing *The Legend of Grizzly Adams,* and several scripts which have been optioned for production.

Tedrow is president of FamilyVision Entertainment Corporation, headquartered at Universal Studios Florida. He lives with his wife, Carla, and their four children, in Winter Park, Florida.